Let The
Dominoes
Fall

ROBERT LAFOND

Inquiries and Book Orders should be addressed to:

Great Writers Media
Email: info@greatwritersmedia.com
Phone: 877-600-5469

ISBN: 978-1-960605-14-6 (sc)
ISBN: 978-1-960605-15-3 (ebk)

Contents

Introduction
Gooseberry Island, RI

On a dark stretch of Narragansett Boulevard, Police find an abandoned Audi. There's blood on the driver's seat and headrest, but there are no signs of an accident and no driver. The next morning a heavy fog engulfs the Bay, as a dory motors out to Gooseberry Island. Two people are in the boat, but one is dead. The dory stops on the rocky pimple and leaves the dead man's body on the island's west side.

Later that day, a U.S. Coast Guard patrol boat finds a body on the tiny island. It has several bullet holes in it. The coroner verifies a .22 caliber weapon was used. The victim was identified as the owner of the abandoned Audi, also the owner of the Western Point Marina.

Within weeks, the bodies of an outdoorsman found off the Lincoln Woods Road and a missing college professor, located on the banks of the Blackstone River near the Old Slater Mill Dam, are added to the cases piling up on Captain January's desk. There is only one similarity; these additional victims were also killed with a .22 caliber weapon.

Prelude

They were high school friends, each with a different personality and idea about tomorrow, unsure of the future.

The day before graduation this tight-knit group from Mt. Valle High is celebrating at Cotter's Drug Store. One of the group, John Roberts, is working behind the counter today. He's the short-order cook who flips the burgers, makes the fries, and whips up Egg Crème sodas and Lime Rickey's. I'm sitting on the last stool at the end of the counter while John and I are listening to our friends talk about their dreams for tomorrow. My name is Grant Smalley.

Rachel Biggar, the class Valedictorian, will be at Harvard this Fall. She wants to climb beyond the case-loaded walls of her father's law firm and work in state government with dreams of the State Capital.

Thomas Florin, the class clown, plans on attending Yale. He wants to jump into politics to straighten out the *mess in Washington.* He should have had that kind of dedication on the Debate Team during the last debate of the year.

Howard Reynolds, bookworm slash writer, dreams of getting on the NY Times Best Seller list. Attending the University of Rhode Island, he drowns in Hemingway, Steinbeck, Waldon, and Longfellow, wondering how much longer the four literary giants will dealy his success. The never thought his low draft number could go into effect until he received an invitation from Uncle Sam. The

Army sent him to Viet Nam for six months, after which he came home wounded and very silent.

Art Williams, the perfect rogue, has all the talent of a Jack-of-all-Trades, yet never mastered anything. Except to say his silver tongue would lead you to believe he was good at everything. It was no surprise when he announced he was going into the Army. We wished him well knowing where he was going. Before the end of Summer Art would be routing out the enemy in the jungles on South VietNam.

John Roberts planned on attending college in Canada, not to avoid the draft. Had a very high number. But he wanted a different perspective on Law and the ethics associated with it.

They were five friends who thought graduation was the end of their lives together. No one could have guessed how much their paths would cross in years to come. I was going to be one of the people to try to straighten out those crossings.

But cross they did; for some, tragically.

CHAPTER 1

Change Coming

While behind the grill, John Roberts tells me of his plans to see some of the country before heading up to Canada and Bittern Law University in Ontario. It wasn't his intent to avoid the draft; he had a high number. A career in political science is his choice of study, emphasizing the ethical and legal limitations. "A change is needed in Washington," he insisted. Everyone paused, then Thom Florin jumped up to offer a toast.

"My friends, this is our last goodbye. We cross that bridge tomorrow with all the tools we need to capture that brass ring and succeed in our endeavors. Good Luck to all." He finalized his speech, 'Salude.'

Art Williams whispers to me, "Where did that bullshit come from?" Then Rachel stood to announce,

"Well done, Thomas. Those were the most profound words you've spoken in four years." We all laughed as she raised her Coke and yelled, 'Salude.'

They were a fun group, but not my regular gang to spend constructive time with. I am a Trades geek, and my friends were Trades geeks; Sam Lewinski, Bill Cannon, and Elliot Cardoza. I'm Grant

Smalley, and my Trade Study is Architectural Design. We walked down a different hallway in the school building, far away from the quiet, conservative intellectuals planning to attend college. Sam was a car nut and took Automotive Studies. Bill had a talent for wood and took Carpentry classes. Elliot was entranced by the study of AC and DC and in which direction they flowed. He enrolled in the Electrical courses. We could design, demolish and build back better almost anything. A year later, I wished we could rebuild our closeness and friendship.

My buddies wanted to serve in the Navy together after high school; the recruiter said they could. But as Sam wrote in one of his letters, "the Navy said it was for the good of the service." The three were separated after Boot Camp, and each was posted according to their aptitude test scores. They never saw one another again.

Sam was aboard a tender off the coast of Cam Ran Bay when an *undefined accident* landed him in the hospital for several months. His Navy career was shattered. They sent him home, telling him, "You're of no use to us anymore." Honorably discharged and given a Purple Heart, the compensation for Sam's injuries did nothing to quell the anger he carried home. Sam lived with his parents until he hooked up with a former girlfriend, Georgia Baker. She was a trauma nurse and helped Sam square away. They married and moved out to another part of the state. It was a lovely wedding.

Bill Canon wrote one letter from Nam, apologizing, "It's all I have time for." He didn't like writing, telling everybody *How it was going,* over there. One letter was graphic and angry. Bill told me what he did, the horror he saw, and the shame he tried to hide. I didn't understand what he was talking about until he told me the Navy shoved him into the Corps and put a machine gun in his hands, telling him to 'go kill bad guys.'

He came home wounded when his tour was over, not telling anyone how it happened. I let it go because conversations with Bill were difficult. Easily agitated and suspicious, he would always look around to see if anyone was following him. His father told me, "It's

PTSD." Bill moved away, telling no one where he was going. I haven't heard from him in a while now.

Elliot 'Cardy' Cardoza became a hero, at least that's how I saw it. The Navy refused his admittance, for some reason, and told him to try the Army. They trained him as a weapons specialist and sent him to Viet Nam only to return home eight months later, sealed in a metal casket. His parents were told Elliot died, saving the lives of his buddies. The commendation read, "though severely wounded, Corporal Cardoza, advanced on the enemy, killing four of them before succumbing to his injuries." There was talk of a grenade, but I didn't pay much attention to it. I only knew my friend was dead.

Elliot's father wept to see the Silver Star and Purple Heart pinned to the folded flag the captain presented to Elliot's mother. The haunting sound of Taps, played with an echo, still rings in my heart when I visit his grave. I see the snap of the soldier's salute, smell the shadowed veil of white smoke as the guns fire, and see Elliot's mom hugging the flag, filling it with her tears.

It's been a year since Elliot's funeral. It wasn't until after I joined the R.I. State Police that I understood the brotherhood soldiers shared; living, working, fighting, and dying, together, so close, so dedicated to one another. Above all others in the cemetery, Elliot's grave will always be the most solemn.

His death left me in a deep funk. My father watched me wade through my breakfast cereal one morning. He told me,

"You've got to dig yourself out of this hole, Grant. You're not doing anyone, especially yourself, any good by dragging your ass around the house."

Sometimes dads make the most sense when you least want them to. Even as a lawyer, my dad's logic sometimes hurts.

That was when I signed with the Rhode Island State Police and entered the Academy when the next class started. I figured it would be a safer way to serve at home than going off to a foreign country, having them shoot at me day and night. The R.I.S.P. put me through the paces for two years, after which I earned a badge, a gun, and a whole lot of respect. During the early years, everything was going great. I was enjoying the job, enjoying the camaraderie of my fellow troopers. My education in criminal studies never stopped, and I was acing all my courses. But after nine years, I felt I needed a change, not one out of law enforcement, but in Law somewhere else.

I searched through newspapers and other Law-type literature at night, looking for something different, still in law, while maintaining my duties as a Trooper during the day. The Chief of Police in a small New Hampshire town caught my eye. I looked it up on a map and found it wasn't that far from home. I found the town's web page and liked everything about it; the pictures were beautiful, the demographics seemed easy to get used to, so I sent in my resume and waited for a letter of acceptance or the form letter of, *"We are sorry to inform you...."*

After two weeks of anticipation and nail-biting, a letter arrived informing me that I had gotten the job. No instructions asked me to appear before a town council for an interview. *"Perhaps," I thought, "it'll be by phone."* I waited for a call, but the one I got surprised me. It was from the New Hampshire State Attorney General. He informed me of a referral from Rachel Biggar, the R.I. State Attorney General.

"That's all we need, mister. Come on up." The AG told me. So, I am now the Police Chief of a sleepy little tourist town on the edge of a big lake.

I look back at where I've been the last ten years, how far I have come, how much was I leaving behind.

"Graduating Mt. Valle, that hot June day, wearing those long hot gowns. I felt I had accomplished something when the principal put that 'Scroll of Success' in my hands. The class voted not to call it a diploma. I laughed at the foolishness at Cotter's Drug Store and Tom Florin, and listened to them talk while Jon flipped burgers and whipped up shakes.

Most of us knew where we were going, I guess; off to college somewhere. But some of the class enlisted and paid the price for service to their country. The class, as a whole, attended a couple of funerals, most with closed casket. From our guilt, some of us did volunteer service that summer. We visited men and women in the hospitals, nursing homes, and those at home in their wheelchairs needing assistance."

Then there was the night I met a man who cared about us high school drunks, Officer Homer January.

"It was 10:00 PM on Friday, and I had just left Rachel Biggar's party, drunk as a skunk. As far as beers are concerned, I found my limit, and now I had to make my way home. Three sheets to the wind themselves, a couple of friends offered me a ride home, but I refused, seeing how far gone they were. I told them, "No, thanks. I'll walk off some of this beer before I get home."

"Okay," and off they went, weaving down the street headed for the Diamond By-Pass. Classmate Eddy Peets was driving, and neighbor Johnny MacLellan was his passenger. Five minutes later, an ambulance, a police cruiser, and a fire truck zoomed past me, going the other way. After another five minutes, a pair of headlights pulled up behind me. It was a police officer with a flashlight. He called out my name,

"Are you Grant Smalley?" he called out.

"Yeah?" I answered.

"Get in the car, son. I'll take you home."

Under diminished capacity, I got in the back seat of the cruiser. Most local gendarmes don't bother picking up kids walking home from a party. They simply lock them up and call their parents. Tonight, other officers were busy at the accident.

"Who are you?" I asked. "Do you know my dad?"

"Yes, I know your father. I'm Officer January. So, you've had a few drinks, huh?"

"Yeah. I don't usually," I confessed. "But I was having a good time. Do you know what happened back there, with the ambulance and the cruiser and the fire truck?"

Officer January paused, then told me, "There was a bad accident. A couple of kids were going too fast on the Diamond By-Pass, didn't make the curve." He didn't tell me the car hit a tree and burst into flames.

"Did they get out? Did they survive?" I asked.

Another pause, but this time it took a little longer. Turning down my street, Officer January stopped, then turned around and told me,

"No, son. There were no survivors."

I went silent, dead inside, and began to weep, thinking, "My friends, Eddy and Johnny, were in that car." I walked up the driveway, with my head bowed down, when Officer January called me back to his car.

"Son, I won't fault you for having fun with your friends at a house party. I did it, too, when I was your age, but the laws are different today regarding the use of alcohol, and the cars are a lot faster," he added.

"You've got to learn to either stop the drinking or accept a ride home from someone who is not drinking."

He then asked me, "Did the driver of that car ask to give you a ride home?"

"Yes," I told him painfully.

"Consider yourself lucky you didn't take it. I'm sorry you lost two friends, but if you had gone with those boys, I would be telling your parents you weren't coming home."

I wanted to scream across the Grand Canyon just to fill the void of silence between us.

Officer January stared and said, "Good night, son."

I've seen Officer Homer January advance to Corporal January, Sergeant January, then Lieutenant January, culminating into Captain Homer January, head of the Homicide Division of the R.I. State Police.

Every time we meet, I thank him for changing my drinking habits and how I've gained a new outlook, especially since becoming a Rhode Island State Trooper. We are friends, but we don't get to see each other often since I've moved to New Hampshire.

Chapter 2

New Adventures

The morning I left Rhode Island was bright and sunny, but my chest felt dark and cold, a vibrating mass of excitement and sorrow inside. I hated to leave all I grew up with, but I wanted to go and experience something new. I walked into the barracks, almost ashamed that I was leaving. I turned in my badge and service pistol, then shook the hands of the men I served alongside. They wished me well, and I promised to visit whenever I was in the area. "I can do that," I told them.

I purchased a new gun for myself, not knowing the requirements in New Hampshire. I stuffed a duffle bag with clothes, a photo of mom and dad and left everything else in my room. New memories were waiting to be made. I had my car in the shop, wanting to make sure it would make the trip, but the mechanic told me it needed serious repairs. I couldn't see spending the money on repairs that were sure to fail, so I traded for a new pick-up.

In the window of an animal rescue shelter stood a drop-jawed pup, up on his hind legs. I spotted him as I was leaving the dealership. We stared at one another as I was driving away. I watched until he was out of sight, but could not let go of that proud face. I turned around, all the while questioning myself, 'Would a dog make a good companion? Did I want, do I need, a little friend like that?' Then a voice in my head chimed in, telling me,

"*Don't do it. You won't have time to care for it. You will be too busy chasing criminals.*" And I thought,

"Wait! How many criminals can there be in New Hampshire?"

If anything, it was curiosity that got me to walk in. I went over to the window and saw the little guy up on two paws trying to get over the glass wall. He wanted someone to pick him up. Was it animal magnetism? Did I feel sorry for him? Maybe a little of both. I turned and asked the clerk,

"How much do you need for me to take this beast home with me?"

"$50," she said. "You also get a heavy link chain, a whip with a barbed end, and one meal of raw meat. How you handle the fire breathing is up to you," and then she laughed.

"I've always wanted to say that." she added, "but I never saw anyone I thought would understand the fun. You look like you understand."

She didn't look any more than 17, but she was cute. I laughed at her comment, then showed her my I.D. as a police officer. My S&W 40 was on my belt. "I think I can handle the beast," I told her.

She reeled back, then stopped and understood my half of the joke.

"Oh! You're a police officer. Well, I guess he's going to learn a few things from you."

We traded $50 cash for a new leash, a twenty-pound bag of dog food, and papers indicating he had all his shots. He was a 12-week-old English Boxer.

"You'll like him," she said. "Thank you for taking him." Then she slapped, an '*I am an Adoption Parent! Woof!*' sticker on my chest.

"Well, that's official enough for me." I picked him up and looked into his eyes. He then welcomed me with warm piddle down the front of my shirt. I looked him in the eyes and said,

"That is the last time you'll ever do that again, buster," and that's how I named him *Buster Piddle.*

I put him on the floor of my cab, and he fell right to sleep. Dog urine is so bad; it's worse than lousy perfume. Off came the shirt. I reached into my duffle and found a box of handi-wipes. 'Mom must have put these in there.'

I wiped down my chest and put on a fresh shirt—the ruined one I tossed in the back of the truck. I wasn't going to smell puppy urine on the way up to Lakes Crossing. I didn't know how long it would take me to get there, so I stopped for drive-through burgers and a shake. Buster kept his head down the whole trip. I felt sure the smell of the burgers would wake him, but I was going to keep him away from human food.

Buster picked his head up as soon as I pulled into the station parking lot. He began scratching at the door, and I knew what that meant. I ran around to the passenger's side before he could relieve himself in the truck. No sooner had his feet hit the pavement, an ocean of yellow began to spread. I backed away so I wouldn't track anything into the station house.

Mission accomplished, I placed the leash on him and led him to the station. He stopped at the first desk, where the Deputy greeted him. For a moment, I thought I saw Buster smile.

"Hey there, little guy. You can't come in here. Didn't you see the sign on the door? Where is your owner." He turned and greeted me, saying,

"Your dog is going to have to wait outside, mister."

"Does that go for the new Chief, too?" I asked.

"Oh, sorry, sir," the Deputy said, stammering all over himself. He was young, mid-twenties, and jumped up into a crisp salute. Then offered a handshake, "Deputy William H. Holiday, sir."

"Bill Holiday, huh? Do you pull teeth or sing, Bill?" I asked. Then introduced myself,

"Grant Smalley. Chief Grant Smalley, now," then I showed him my I.D.

"You know your stuff, Billie?" I asked.

"Proudly, sir. Yes, sir, I do. What do you need, sir?"

I looked around the office, surveying the 'ambiance of law' décor, cold gray, no hint of discernable color. *This place looks like a morgue. That is going to change,* I said to myself.

"Can I get a cup of coffee, Billy? Two sugars, two creams?"

"Yes, sir,"

"I'll be in my office."

A tall man in a Police uniform was just leaving my office.

"Hello," I said, staring at 6'4" of form-fitting NH State Police uniform. He wore captain's bars on his collar. I offered my hand.

"I'm the new Chief, Grant Smalley, and you are…."

"Captain Norman Butler, New Hampshire State Police, Forensics. Welcome." He had a healthy handshake with big, meaty hands. I found that confidence building, and I felt good about it. He spotted Buster and said to him,

"Aren't you the handsome one?" Norm offered his hand, and Buster raised his paw in return.

"Very good, young fella. What do you have for a name?"

"This is Buster Piddle; I'll explain that later. Do you have a dog, Norm?"

"Three. My hound works with the State as a tracker, a particularly good one, too, I'm proud to say. My other two are play dogs, a Border Collie and a Dachshund. Odd pair, I know, but they get along, and I have fun with them. Rescued all three."

"Nice thing to do," I said. "That's how I got Buster. I don't know why people take them in if they're not going to care for them." I shuffled a few papers on the desk and asked,

"What brings Forensics to Lakes Crossing?"

"You had a death last week. A young lady fell down a flight of stairs in her home. She did not look the type to take a fall. She wasn't old, feeble, or disabled in any way, a former cheerleader with a very shapely figure. But she hit her head on the cement floor, and that was it. Until the coroner told me he found something. I told him a new chief was on the way, so he wanted to wait until you arrived to finish the report."

"Wow. I'm not here an hour, and I've got a murder case on my hands." I commented.

"Well, I don't know if it's a murder case just yet, but the coroner makes it sound suspicious," Norm added. "Do you feel like a ride to Concord? I'll buy supper." he offered.

"Might as well delve right into it," I told him. "Billie, your first duty is to watch Buster. Take him out every two hours, or he will take you out. I don't want to find a mess in the station."

CHAPTER 3

1st Case

It was late afternoon when we arrived at the morgue. Sandy Reynolds would be my first conversation with a dead person. I had not seen her husband yet, but I didn't need his permission; this was all part of the investigation.

Norm described Sandy Reynolds as a beautiful, young, red-headed woman in the prime of her life, the early thirties.

'You were supposed to be building your future young lady,' I thought, *'not getting ready to lie in your grave.'*

I told Norman I knew the husband, Howard Reynolds, that we were classmates at Mt. Valle. He and Sandy moved to New Hampshire ten years ago. I didn't think he would have changed much. Though I hadn't seen him in all this time, I would probably still recognize him.

The morgue was cold, not unlike an early winter morning, and painted a two-tone gray, uninviting, but then, who wants to be invited to a morgue? The M.E. opened the freezer door and rolled Sandy Reynolds out for viewing. Pulling the sheet back, I could see she was, or used to be, the vivacious redhead Norm described. She had maintained her college cheerleader figure but was now a shadow of the woman she used to be. Her hair faded into the shade of a late summer sunset, difficult to describe.

The medical examiner said she died from more than a fall or a blow to the head.

"How do you mean, Doc?" Norman asked.

He rolled the body to one side and gave us a view of a pinhole in the back of her neck.

"Someone injected her with a fast-acting sedative before letting her fall down the stairs," he told me, "She was unconscious, or more likely dead before she hit the cement."

Now we know it's a murder case, but who do I charge? The husband is always first on the list, and so far, there are no other suspects.

"Do you know what the drug was?" I asked.

"Just got the results. This guy wanted her out of the way, that's for sure. He mixed Hydroxyzine and Ativan. She never had a chance, even if she had survived the fall. She would have been dead in a matter of seconds."

"Thanks for waiting for us, Doc," Norm told him.

We stopped for supper on the way home and discussed the case and what I would do with Howard Reynolds.

"It doesn't make any sense," I told Norm. "The man's a writer, not a murderer. I seriously doubt he knows anything of chemistry to be able to pick out the right drug, and I don't think he'd even know where to get it," I reasoned.

Norm agreed. "Uh-huh. Of course, he could always look it up, research the library, or even the Internet. But, in the end, you still have to charge someone with murder," he added, and Howard Reynolds was it. I hated to do it, but I had to arrest a fellow graduate from Mt. Valle.

Billie and I drove out to Reynolds' house early the following day. I knocked on the door.

"Howard Reynolds, it's Chief of Police, Grant Smalley. Open up."

I gave Reynolds a chance to find his slippers and robe. It was only a minute before he came to the door.

"Yes?" Reynolds questioned.

"Howard Reynolds, you are under arrest for the murder of one, Sandy Reynolds."

"Grant Smalley? Are you living up here, too?" he asked.

"Yes, Howard, but we will have to renew old acquaintances later. Right now, I have a job to do. Would you turn around?"

"You know me, Grant. I'm not a murderer."

"Well, that might be true, Howard, but that's fodder for another book. You can call a lawyer when we get to the station."

Reynolds looked like a lost soul on a deserted island. He jumped when the cell door closed and cringed at the sound of the lock. I retrieved a portable phone and told him to call his lawyer.

"Can I call long distance?" he asked.

"Just make it short and to the point, Howard. I'm not about to pay your lawyer's fees."

"Thank you," he whispered in dismay.

The lawyer showed up the following morning, driving up from Providence. He was a weasely little guy from the law firm of Shasta and Bowe. A young attorney in a new firm, Jeffrey Bowe was one of the founding partners. He was the prosecutor against which my father fought while defending the accused. Never having met him, I looked forward to it when he came to see his client, my prisoner.

Atty. Bowe was waiting in my office the following day. I pulled into my parking slot and walked over to the Mercedes parked in the handicapped zone.

"Nice Benz," I said, glaring at the little guy with the briefcase. "Is that yours?"

"Yes," said a prideful Jeffrey Bowes. "You like it?"

"Yes, but I'm going to ask you to move it. You are in a handicapped zone."

"But there were no other cars in the lot?" he pleaded.

"Well, I put a ticket on your car because you parked in a handicapped area. Now, if you don't pay the fine, your car will be towed. I think you know what that means."

Bowe went out to move his car, thinking I was bluffing about the ticket until he found it on his windshield. He moved his shiny, black Mercedes to an unmarked slot and came back in the office huffing and puffing about it.

"This is outrageous. $100 for a parking violation? I won't pay it." He raged.

"Okay. Billie, call the towing company." I said point-blank.

"No, wait. I just came to see my client!" he insisted.

"Look, Mr. Bowe," I looked him in the eye. "I come from Providence. I attended the R.I. State Police Academy. I know what the law is in R.I. regarding tickets that go unpaid. You and I both know the price of retrieval from impound is high. The fine for an unpaid parking ticket is high. Now, would you agree you are getting off rather cheaply by comparison?"

The little four-foot ten-inch weasel white-knuckled his brief-case, and with a big sigh, confessed,

"Yes, I would agree." He produced a personal check and wrote it out for the fine. He insisted on a receipt, so I had Billie write him one.

I offered, "You can pass that on to your client in his bill."

To rub salt in the wound, I offered my hand as Jeffrey Bowe walked into my office.

"I'm Chief Grant Smalley. You can see your client now."

Billie escorted Bowes to Reynolds' cell. When Billie returned, he told me, "He's still fuming."

"Let him burn. The little bastard thinks he can break the law because he's a lawyer. He can take that receipt to Providence. They'll laugh at him."

I was at my desk enjoying my coffee when Bowe walked in after two hours with his client. He offered his hand, saying, "Jeffrey Bowe, attorney for Mr. Howard Reynolds. Sorry I was such a prick. Now that the formalities are out of the way, how much is the bail?"

"Ah, as much as I would like to be the one to determine that amount, I'm afraid you'll have to ride to Concord with Billie to see the judge. He'll tell you what he thinks Howard's bail should be."

Billie drove Reynolds in the Crown Vic Cruiser while Jeffrey Bowe followed in his Mercedes. The judge would decide if bail was appropriate for Howard Reynolds. If Bowe is smart, he'll play his cards with some intelligence and not the wise little shit he played before me. I hoped the judge would do good for Howard. Just as they left, Norm Butler came in.

"Bail hearing today?"

"Yeah. I hope the judge doesn't hit John too hard."

"Hey, Arthur Percy is on the bench today. He and I go way back. I'll give him a call and tell him what's up on the case." Norm offered.

"Well, that's nice of you to do that, Norm."

The switchboard at the courthouse was unattended. The operator picked it up just as Norm was getting ready to hang up.

"Nancy, where you been?"

"Oh, hi, Norm, potty break. What can I do for you?"

"Has Judge Percy taken the bench yet?"

"Just getting his robe on now."

"Can you rush in and tell him I must speak with him, briefly."

"Okay." Nancy returned with Arthur Percy in tow.

"Norman, what are you doing interrupting my proceedings? I've got people to hang."

"Lakes Crossing has sent down a Howard Reynolds, with his lawyer, for a bail hearing. I'm on the case with the Chief up here, and we have no evidence that proves the man is guilty or innocent. He just happened to be the only one at the scene. Can you take it easy on the bail? This guy doesn't have a pot to piss in. He's a fellow high school graduate with the Chief here and the A.G. in Providence."

"He knows Rachel Biggar? Well, I guess I can do the fellow a favor. I want to know, Norm, how that case comes out if I'm not presiding over it."

"You've got it, Arthur. I'll stop in and let you know. Don't tell his lawyer what we're doing. That little shit needs to see New Hampshire law. Thanks again."

CHAPTER 4

The January Process

Every morning, the question of where I start stares me in the face. I come to work, hoping to close out one case a day. The phone was ringing when I got to my door. State Police Commissioner David Albright was throwing questions at me about three dead Marines and an escaped prisoner.

"You have to close these cases, Homer, as fast as possible. I can't have the entire Marine Corps knocking on my door looking for answers or going out trying to solve these cases themselves."

Albright did not appreciate that kind of phone call starting his day, and neither did I.

"I'm working on the first two, Dave, but I've got no clues."

"Start with the fact they're Marines, Homer," he suggested.

"But they're all out of the Corps. It's better than chasing ghosts, I guess. Once the shit hits the fan, it never stops." Homer added, *"I'll get back to you if I get anything new."*

"That was the last time I talked to him. Three men, all ex-Marines, were all killed with a .22. Why does this thing sound like organized crime? A .22? Mafia? They haven't been active in the city for over 20 years. There was not one damn clue at any scene, not a single shell casing. Then why did I feel these cases were connected?

The escaped convict, John Roberts? That case was a separate animal, altogether. He escaped from a Canadian prison. Why would anyone want him assassinated? I don't have to worry now about deporting him back to Canada. He's dead, and they don't want him. But what do I do with the body? The Canadian authorities figured he came from the U.S. and died in the U.S.; bury him in the U.S.

The Marine murders? They had to be planned, a simple plan, maybe, but plotted out for sure. Nobody shoots three Marines on a whim; you make mistakes, and then you wind up being a target. The killer must have followed them at night. How else could he get to them?

And the Roberts shooter would have needed a high perch. They have to be two separate cases. There are enough similarities in the Marine cases to link them, but nothing connects Roberts to that case. He wasn't even a Marine.

I saw no reason to handle them any other way but separately. With no witnesses to the Marine shootings, no one saw anything; no one heard anything. Yet the killer, or killers, knew where these guys were and at the right time.

Roberts had to have a snitch; somebody told the shooter what time Roberts would be there. If I find the snitch, I'll find the killer. The State, or maybe the Feds, will take care of the body. The Marine by the dam? Why not just push him in, let nature do its thing. The college professor, well, nature got the best of him.

And the body the Coast Guard found on that tiny island didn't make any sense at all. What did it mean? Did it have anything to do with the Marina expansion, or did a pissed-off neighbor just want to get even? But I know that neighborhood; killers don't live there. The two shots to the head tie the three victims together, but why? How? And how does the shooter know when and where these guys are when he kills them?

Albright's suggestion may have been my best first shot, starting with their association to the Corps. I found they all served in the

Middle East as snipers, but at different times. Was someone from the Muslim community trying to get even with the Corps.? It seemed a stretch, but I put a man on it anyway. I've been chasing criminals for almost 20 years, but these cases are driving me nuts. I've got a body here and a body there, and not one damn clue at any of the crime scenes. As a former Marine, I'm taking it personally.

Snipers like to shoot, but did they shoot around here? They weren't hunters, according to their wives and neighbors. But they did brag about their trophies, so they enjoyed competing. Now I have to find out where they competed. The phone book gave me one club in South Kingston, and one of the wives gave me a photo of the three men together. "Now, I might be getting somewhere."

They traveled to South Kingston to compete, so they knew one another. Maybe not personally, possibly just best buds, but they knew one another. There were successes and failures all the way around. Marriages, divorces, kids, and plenty of bills, but what called for their assassination? Going through my list of useless scribbles, all I had to go on was the Crosshairs Sportsmen and Gun Club. I called and got a sweet-sounding gal to say hello.

"Good morning, Crosshairs Sportsmen and Gun Club. My name is Sherry; how can I help you today?"

"Good morning, Sherry; this is Captain Homer January of the Rhode Island State Police. I need to know if you have three men as members of your Club. Can you help me with that?"

"Well, I'm not supposed to give information about the members."

"Miss, you don't want me to come down there with a warrant, do you? That would be very embarrassing to the Club. All you have to do is tell me if they are members."

After a slight pause, she replied,

"Oh, alright. I certainly don't want to cause any embarrassment to the Club. Can you give me their names, Captain?"

I gave her the names verified through our records and the victim's wives. She said,

"Yes. They are members."

"How long have they been with the club?"

She said, "*Three years.*"

"*Did they compete much?*" I asked.

"*Every competition the Club sponsored, it looks like.*"

"Thank you, Sherry," and I hung up the phone. Now I was getting somewhere and had reason to visit the Club and find out what the Marines were doing.

CHAPTER 5

A Re-acquaintance

John Roberts left his job at Cotter's before the summer ended. He wanted to do some traveling before heading north to college. Arriving in Ontario, Canada, he entered Bittern Law University in time for the first semester. With Politics, Governance, and Ethics wrapped around the Law, he hoped to understand the whys' and wherefores' of being President of a large nation, like the United States or Canada.

At home, the President was messing up the country, and the people were rising in protests in every major city, coast to coast, and calling for his ouster. Jack felt ashamed to be a US citizen, and he wanted to do something about it.

"Why would the President want to take away the people's health care system? What does the fool hope to accomplish? The plan he's proposing has been proven not to work. And where is the help the government is supposed to send people in those areas hit by natural disasters? He refuses to send them aid money unless they bend down and kiss his feet, swear allegiance, make him king. Well, maybe not actually, but figuratively."

Believing the upcoming election would be difficult for the current Administration, favored Senators and Congressmen were backing him with every dirty, unethical trick in the book. The President adamantly opposes the Democratic party winning the election and fears they would destroy the country with their left-wing, off-center ideology. Some believed he wouldn't vacate the White House if he lost. That would be a massive wound on the Government and challenging to heal.

The Republican party was heavily involved in gerrymandering all over the country. Voting districts were becoming difficult for black and brown people to vote in. House Democrats were fighting with every tool they had to stem the tide of those tricks, while Comstock's people were salting the airwaves and newspapers with false stories of Democratic dealings within the party. They were printing outright lies of favoritism, voting irregularities, and accusing them of stealing votes in highly favored Republican districts.

Some leading Republicans were revealing the innermost private activities of their opponents in attempts to smear them into surrendering their seats or face expulsion, prosecution, and imprisonment. Tantamount to blackmail, the threats stopped after eliminating certain Senators and Congressmen from Comstock's Cabinet. Law enforcement was at their wit's end, searching for whoever was pulling the trigger.

The people cried out, "The President is not doing his job. He's not protecting and serving, defending, or following the Constitution as written. He swore an oath, and he has broken it for his enrichment. "

"Impeach Him!" they shouted. "Impeach him!"

"Throw him out of office."

But the people would have to wait until November for change to occur. Jack graduated from Bittern Law after six years of complex study and with honors. His last stop before leaving for home was the office of the Dean of Studies. They asked him to go right in without waiting. Jack's political views came right to the fore in the Dean's office. The Dean told him,

"I recognize your outspokenness, young man, and I applaud your willingness to get out there and make a difference. BUT! We here at Bittern would appreciate more discretion and being watchful and attentive to what you are getting involved in. For God's sake, man, try to stay out of trouble. It would not look good for Bittern or you."

"Do you understand, Mr. Roberts?"

Jack didn't know how to answer him. Feeling like he was on trial, his legal studies were now failing him. He kept his reply simple.

"Yes, Sir. I understand. I will do my best to bring credit to Bittern Law. I want to thank you and the faculty, professors, and staff, for allowing me to achieve the Honor of being a Bittern Law graduate."

Jack went back to the States through Watertown, New York, hoping to catch up with a friend he met during his travels. On the run from collectors, Ed Hayner viewed an apartment in the less-than-ideal east side of the city. The owner and landlord, a small, burly, slightly bent man, met him at the front of the building.

"Well, I hope it looks a little better on the inside than it does on the outside," he thought to himself.

"Looks like a squatter's apartment," he commented loudly.

"Funny, that's what the other tenant called it, too. I try to keep it up, and the city hasn't closed me down yet."

Ed was surprised the man could hear him in his whispers. *"The only endearing part of this transaction is going to be the rent,"* he told himself.

"I need to rent it, son. The city doesn't want to see empty buildings and apartments while some people are still sleeping in the streets." The landlord also explained that the city offered a subsidy for available apartments.

"So that's why the rent is so low. I have to admit, seventy-five a week ain't bad." He looked around, assessing his investment, trying to find a way to chip a little bit off the rent.

"Would you take sixty-five, and I'll help you take care of the place?"

The little man scratched his chin, spitting a wad of tobacco into the sink. Jake looked in the sink, *"So that accounts for the nasty color and the smell."*

The landlord agreed to Ed's deal.

"Alright, that's a deal. I'll get some furniture in here for you."

They shook hands when Ed asked one more question.

"A security deposit?"

The man looked around and laughed. "Are you kidding, son? No, no security, just the sixty-five."

Ed handed him the money and told the man he would help him bring in any furniture he had. The man's son would be around in a few minutes to help bring it up from cellar storage.

"Boy, I'm glad I got the first floor."

Ed and the landlord's son, who looked a lonesome forty, brought up several pieces of furniture for the dining room, living room, and bedroom. Small appliances, linens, and curtains were Ed's responsibility, but the son told him he might be able to locate a couple of sets of curtains from one of the other vacant apartments. In an hour, there was some civility to the place.

He dropped down on the well-worn sofa, thinking he might get a little sleep when the doorbell rang. Jumping up in surprise, "Who the hell is ringing the doorbell? No one is supposed to know I'm here." He made his way to the window to see Jack Roberts standing at the door.

"Jack Roberts? What the hell are you doing here? I thought you were busy working on some law degree in Ontario?"

"Well, that was six years ago. I graduated, and now I'm making my way home to see mom and start making a life." Jack strolled through the apartment, feigning admiration, commenting on the shapes and colors on the walls. "Modern art, Eddy?" he asked facetiously.

"Smartass!" Ed called him." I don't have your bread, Jack; you know that."

"But I thought you were hitting it big with the electronics thing and the store you had going. What happened? This is a far cry from the last place you were living." Jack then took two 50-dollar bills from his wallet and gave them to Ed.

"What's this?" Ed asked. "You don't have to do this, Jack."

"As you said, Eddy, *you don't have my bread.*' Besides, I can get more."

"What happened was, I got mixed up with another John Roberts. Can you believe that?"

"Get out, another me?" Jack said in astonishment.

"No, not another you, Jack. This guy was a bit daring. We had the store, and it was great while we had something to sell. Then we lost everything when trends changed. Product was flying off the shelves, which was great, but I couldn't restock. I couldn't buy any new stuff coming out; it was too expensive. So, when we closed the store, my partner, John Roberts, decided he wanted to print his own money. Don't you know he got caught trying to pass a phony Canadian note at a border store? The Canadian Government gave him five years, which was the last time I saw him. I thought they were going to come after me."

"So, now you're on the run from collectors and maybe the Canadian government. That's why you're living like this?" Jack summarized.

"Bingo."

"I'm sorry, Ed. I had no idea things were that bad. I was studying my ass off in school, trying to find a way to depose that 'man who would be king' in Washington. Boy, does he piss me off?"

"He's in Washington, Jack. That's politics. Leave him alone; the people will straighten him out at the next election."

"But he's killing people, Ed, with his policies and crazy laws he keeps passing. Many of them are illegal, and people die before any corrections can take effect. The man's a killer, Ed, and he doesn't even care. He has got to be stopped."

"Well, if you feel that strongly about it, there is a political rally tonight, downtown. There are flyers all over the city, and I heard the cops are getting ready if there's any trouble. Lots of my friends are going. I might go," Ed offered.

"Do you want to go?"Ed asked.

"Who's on the podium?" Jack asked.

"Some guy from Providence is supposed to show up."

"What the hell is he doing here in Watertown?"

"I heard he's a State Senator with his eye on the White House. He's got some crazy ideas with a whole generation of young people behind him."

"Well, he might be worth a listen. I think I'll go and see what this guy is all about."

"Okay, then. I'll go with you. Maybe we'll get to see the Oval Office." Jack got the inference and thought it was funny.

"Yeah, we remove the idiot, and the crowds will force the collapse of the government," he added.

"I don't know if anything will happen that way, Jack. Changes in the Government don't happen that fast unless you're a third-world country. Let's hear what this Senator has to say, first."

They drove out to Kostyk Field, where 5,000 people had gathered to hear Senator Thomas Florin of Rhode Island speak on the use of 'measured resistance' to take back the White House, Congress, the Attys. General's office, and if necessary, even the Supreme Court.

"Lack of consideration for the people, in those areas of greatest need, where governmental assistance can ease the burden, reduce the pain, and bring a stable economy to the area; when the cries go unanswered, then harsh measures and action on the part of the people are called for," Florin said. *"I can not elaborate on that last part. It could result in being thrown in jail for inciting insurrection to overthrow the Government. But that may well be what is needed."*

Ed and Jack listened to the crowd yelling, hollering, and getting worked up. The two weren't sure they wanted to join in. A banner posted on the way into the rally read, ***Let the Dominoes Fall,***"Barkers near the front entrance were selling T-shirts imprinted with the picture of dominoes falling on the back of the shirt and the phrase on the front. They were selling for $40 bucks apiece.

As they listened to the crowd, they looked at one another and thought, *"…a rallying cry?"*

"But in this economy, he may not sell very many of them," Jack told Ed.

"I can tell you what is wrong, but I don't have to. You can see what is wrong, feel what is wrong. Your pockets and the shelves in your homes are empty. In your communities, businesses are shuttered, with no guaranty they will ever re-open. The next election is not that far away. You must make sure you get out and cast your vote. Do it early, tell your friends, but get out there and make a difference. Do we hope the next election will correct all the mistakes? Or do we take action and guarantee the band-aide we apply will stop the bleeding. The people need to apply their compress on the wound to make the dominoes fall in Washington."

After an hour, Jack said, "I know that guy, Ed. I went to high school with him. We were on the same debate team together." Jack watched the crowd hit the concession stand and drop the $40 bucks on the shirt. He was deciding if he wanted one for himself.

"No kidding. You know a State Senator, especially one that wants to take over the Government. I'm impressed. I wonder which domino will fall first." Ed commented.

"Not too loud, buddy. People might not be ready for that kind of stuff." Jack said. "I want to try to reach him, talk to him. I know he'll remember me."

The Senator saw Jack waving at him from the crowd.

"Wait!" Thom instructed his driver. He rolled the window down and yelled, "Jack...Jack Roberts?" he called out. "Get in the car, Jack." Ed chased after them, but Thom told the driver to keep going. He caught a glimpse of the bumper sticker on the back of the Lincoln. It contained a row of dominoes falling, pointing to the White House. *So, it is his rallying cry,* he told himself? *"Yeah...Let the Dominoes Fall."*

CHAPTER 6

Wrong-Way Out

After escaping from the Ottawa-Carleton Detention Center in Ottawa, Ontario, Canada, a winded John Roberts knocked on Ed Hainer's door. Law enforcement throughout Canada and the East Coast of the U. S. were on alert. John was hoping his past business partner might help him out. He found Ed Hainer less than accommodating.

"You want money from me? After what you did? You've got nerve, almost had me sitting in prison with you. You do know I'm still on the run, don't you?"

"Hey, you're the one who gave me the best printer on the market."

"Not for printing money, ass-hole!" Ed said pointedly.

"Okay, I'm sorry, but I'm out, and now I'm on the run. Can you help me out?"

"Why are you out? I thought they gave you five years."

"I escaped this morning," John admitted.

"How do you expect me to help you, John? I don't have any money." Ed lied. He still had the two fifties Jack gave him.

"Nuts!" Ed screamed. "If they trace you here, I'll be up shit's creek, too. You absolutely cannot stay here, John. You need money, but I can't help you." He paced the floor, thinking.

"Wait. I heard somebody talking about a retired guy not far from here. He helps people out sometimes. They say he's got cash stored in every corner of the house. Maybe you can ask him for help."

With that, Ed pushed John out the door, telling him,

"Now, get out of here before somebody sees the two of us together."

John visited the man but didn't spend a lot of time asking for money. Knocking him unconscious, he took the old man's wallet, car keys, and the license plate off his car. He stole a used car off a dealer's lot and headed south to Providence.

The old gent was able to get himself up and call the police. Describing John in his prison clothes, authorities immediately recognized who assaulted the old man, escaped convict John Roberts. He planned to hop a freighter and head into international waters, but he never realized the bread crumbs he was leaving behind at every stop he made.

His first bread crumb was at the used car lot and the car he stole. The second crumb was at the gas station and paying the clerk with a 50 dollar bill for twenty dollars worth of fuel when the clerk noticed John had a twenty in his hands.

"I know I have a twenty, but I need to break the 50," John told the clerk, who, at 20 years old, was not going to argue the transaction. She was afraid John was going to hurt her. After he left, she called her boss.

John dropped his third crumb at an all-night convenience store after giving the clerk his second 50 dollar bill. The clerk asked John to buy a few more items even though John only wanted a pack of gum.

"If I break your fifty on a pack of gum, I'll have no change for other customers. Would you please purchase something else?"

"What is it with you all-night stop guys? You can never break a fifty. Alright, I'll look around."

John saw a hot dog steamer turning. "How old are the dogs?" John asked.

"About an hour. They don't last long." The clerk told him.

John picked up two hot dogs with buns, a can of Coke, and a pack of Twinkies. He went to the counter and dropped down a ten-dollar bill. "It shouldn't cost any more than that," he told the clerk. The clerk added the purchase at the register and found it didn't. He ran out to give John a receipt and his change, but he was already gone. The clerk noted the license on the car was hanging on one screw.

John found a map in the glove box. *"Someone has already plotted a route to Providence!"* he thought. *"There's a port there; I'll find a ship and get out into International waters."* John's third crumb was about to lead him into the hands of the R.I. State Police.

Chief January checked on all the freighters docked in Providence. Only one was set to leave later that morning. His men were positioned north and south of the pier. Another unit would be watching for any vehicle coming onto the dock, any vehicle with only one male passenger.

John stopped to check his map and noticed several cars parked on the far end of the parking lot. He thought nothing of them. *"Early morning stow-aways?"* He thought.

Suddenly, the night sky was awash in flashing blue lights. The number of them lit the night as if it were daytime. He watched the vehicles surround him, then heard,

"John Roberts, get out of the car with both hands above your head."

"Shit! I guess I won't be going any farther tonight," he told himself. Kicking the door open, John stuck both hands out, yelling, "Don't shoot, I'm not armed."

"Both hands above your head and on your knees!" an officer ordered. Three officers ran to John as soon as he was down. One officer handcuffed him and presented him to Captain Homer January.

John gave a resigned grin at the 6'4" police captain staring down at him. He then asked,

"How did you guys know I was coming here? I didn't tell anybody."

"You had nowhere else to go. You're in Indian territory, mister. This is foreign soil for you. What I want to know is why did you pick Providence? Boston was practically a straight shot for you."

"The map," John told him. "It was already highlighted on the map."

"Uh-huh. By the way, that old man you clobbered, the one whose wallet you stole? You hit him pretty good. He's dead. Now you're looking at a murder charge."

"I didn't mean to kill him, just knock him out."

"Then the kid in the gas station, passing a $50 bill, so early in the morning. This wasn't your best day, bud. You should have made sure the screws on the license plate were tight. The clerk at the convenience store saw the plate was hanging by one screw after running out with the receipt and your change."

"Yeah. I left in a hurry. I wanted to eat the dogs while they were still hot, and I didn't need a receipt," John explained.

"I have to admit," Homer told him, "Heading for the coast and hopping a freighter? That was a good idea, getting out of the country, but we had Boston covered, too, just in case."

"Well," John sighed. "I'm tired of running anyway. I just had to get out of that Canadian sewer."

The Donald W. Wyatt Detention Facility in Central Falls, R.I., was built to house individuals who might threaten the general public. John Roberts would be its next guest, temporarily, anyway. A judge would decide what to do with him. Would he be deported to Canada or handed over to New York authorities? The Feds would handle the interstate transportation of a stolen motor vehicle.

Atty. Ralph Smalley got a call from AG Biggar's office that his firm has been assigned to represent an escaped convict sitting in the Wyatt Center. Ralph drove to Central Falls to see this new client. The paperwork on Roberts had not been completed, but he walked the corridor to John's cell with the Correctional Officer, anyway. The jailer announced,

"You got a lawyer, Roberts."

John stood up and made himself presentable to his attorney. He extended his hand to say hello, and Ralph took it as a sign of a good working relationship.

"My name is Ralph Smalley. I have a practice in Providence, and I am hoping you are my last client." Ralph looked at John, trying to put Roberts' face with the John 'Jack Rabbit' Roberts that graduated Mt. Valle. Ralph was given a very crude, quickly made-up rap sheet on John.

"This says you were born in Oregon. How did you end up out here?"

"I wanted to see the country," he laughed.

Digging for his legal pad, Ralph told Roberts,

"I plan on retiring, right after giving the courts holy hell on your behalf. So, let's have as much truth as you have in you, okay."

John smiled at the statement, "*Give the courts holy hell,*" Hmph! Trying to get a guilty man off is like trying to put the cookie back in the jar. It'll be fun to watch."

"You don't know me, son. If you mock my abilities, you won't have the pleasure. I can recommend a lawyer with far less experience if you like." Ralph said in a low bark, with some volume.

"No, I'm sorry. No offense."

Ralph looked at John and pulled out his legal yellow pad. Then told him,

"You talk, I'll write. Anytime you're ready."

John pulled out a pack of cigarettes.

"Do you mind if I smoke?" he asked his attorney.

Ralph told him, "No," then pulled a Cuban Matador cigar from a leather pouch. A gold lighter came out with an 'R/S' script on the side. Ralph went to offer John a light for his cigarette but stopped short. He pulled another cigar from the pouch and clipped the end, then offered it to his client. John's eyebrows went up with his smile. He took the cigar, sniffed it, end to end, then gave Ralph a big grin. A large blue flame arose from the lighter, and the two sat back for a moment. Hitting a buzzer on the table, the guard came in. Ralph asked him,

"Can you bring me a pot of your most excellent roast…and two cups? We are going to be here a while." The two men smiled at one another, then began putting a defense together. He told John,

"I love teasing the jailer. He always says the same thing, the same way." Ralph admitted.

The jailer responded,

"Right. Two cups of coffee."

CHAPTER 7

Bad Jacket

An F.B.I. file came across Rachel Biggar's desk. The headline on the jacket read, 'John Roberts.' Rachel jumped back from the file, thinking,

"John Roberts, from Mt. Valle? John 'Jack Rabbit' Roberts? Why would the F.B.I. have a file on John?" She flipped the file open and was struck by the photo. *"That is not the John Roberts I know."*

After reading the file, Rachel was convinced it was not the same John Roberts from Mt. Valle. The file contained inconclusive testimony from witnesses claiming to have been victims of several bank robberies throughout the Midwest. Descriptions of the perpetrators varied so much; police sketch artists could not develop a good composite image. Yet when shown to the victims, they all said, 'it looks like him, it does.' There were no fingerprints at any of the crime scenes. Weapons were brandished but never fired. Masks were worn, and the robbers were insistent but polite.

Descriptions by all the victims of all the robbers were the same. A lineup of photos resulted in no matches. Stories started circulating of the murders of friends and lovers of this supposed John Roberts. They betrayed him and paid the price for that betrayal. Country folk living in the hills and plains started calling him 'Robin Hood' because he gave them the stolen money for helping him evade capture.

"This thing reads more like Bonnie and Clyde," Rachel told herself, *"But where's Bonnie? And he gets away, scot-free, every time. It can't be the same Jack Rabbit Roberts I know."*

Rachel thought back to when John got the nickname 'Jack Rabbit.' John told her,

"Well, me and daddy used to go rabbit hunting. I didn't carry a gun; I was too small; daddy did. Every time he spotted a rabbit, he would tell me to chase it down. So off I'd go, running hither and yon, chasing after it."

"Did you ever catch one?" Rachel asked.

"Yep, sometimes, I did. They'd be so tuckered out; they would just give up. Daddy would say, 'You are just like a jackrabbit, boy,' and he started calling me 'Jack Rabbit.'"

Rachel called Jack's mother in East Providence.

"Mrs. Roberts, this is Rachel Biggar. How are you, dear? Do you remember me? I am a friend of Jack's from high school."

"Oh, Rachel. Yes, I remember you. John spoke very highly of you."

Rachel asked, "Have you heard from Jack lately?"

"Not within the last month." She replied. "My last letter, he was in Ontario getting ready to graduate college. I believe he may be on his way home. Oh, I'm so proud of him."

"Yes, yes, we all are. If I leave you my number, would you let me know the next time you hear from Jack? I must speak with him. Would you do that for me?"

"Surely. I can do that for you, Rachel."

"Thank you, dear. Bye, now."

The final blow was reading the last page, Jack's capture and imprisonment in Canada, *'Trying to pass counterfeit money at a border crossing.'* John was sentenced to five years at the Ottawa-Carleton Detention Center in Ottawa, subject to be released in two years. Rachel had enough and wouldn't read anymore. She placed a call to the Detention Center. *"Where did you go wrong, Jack? Did you go wrong?"*

"Good morning, Ottawa-Carleton Detention Center. This is Harmony; how can I help you."

"Harmony, this is United States Attorney General Rachel Biggar, from Providence, Rhode Island. Can you tell me if you have an inmate by the name of John Roberts?"

"Well, mam, we did until this morning. He escaped," the receptionist told her.

"He escaped this morning?"

"Yes, or sometime in the night. I was just putting his file back. Was there something you needed to know about him?"

"Yes. Can you tell me his date of birth and where he was born?"

"Let me check…John Michael Roberts, born on April 1st, 1954, in Baker City, Oregon. Anything else I can help you with?"

"Yes. Can you tell me, is there a next of kin listed?"

"His mother died in childbirth. His father committed suicide. No brothers or sisters listed. No one named as a beneficiary to his estate, belongings, or his remains".

"Is there anything else, mam?"

"No, Harmony. Thank you. That's all I need. I appreciate your help." Rachel hung up the phone blowing out a sigh of relief.

"If they had one John Roberts, whose statistics don't match the stats on my John Roberts, and this jacket doesn't mirror either of them, who put this piece of garbage together?"

Senator Florin was not aware Jonathan Adams was a confidant to Rachel. She led Jon to be employed at Florin's office because she wanted someone to monitor the Senator's activities. He was getting proof of the Senator's less than honorable behavior, but his first job was secretary to Thomas Florin.

Rachel called back a few days later, asking to speak to Jonathan.

"This is Jonathan. How can I help you this morning?"

"Jonathan, it's Rachel. Don't go loud on me. I'm just a constituent right now. Please meet me at Crusty's during your lunch hour. Can you make time?"

"Yes, mam. I can do that for you. Expect the information in the mail." Jon then whispered, "I'll see you at 12:30."

"Thank you, Jon."

Crusty's Bakery was just a short walk down to the Providence Place Mall. Jon walked in and made his way around to the last booth where Rachel was waiting.

"Jonathan," she called.

"Hi, Rachel. How are you today?"

"Puzzled, Jon. Has your boss been doing any digging into individuals from Mt. Valle?"

"I don't know. A couple of days ago, he asked me to hand Tippy an envelope, so I did. I didn't open the envelope. I don't know what it contained. I gave it to dad that night. What's going on?"

"This file was on my desk this morning. Did it come across yours?"

"No, I never saw it before. I know the name on the file, John Roberts. Wasn't he a graduate of Mt. Valle?"

"Yes. '*A*' John Roberts came from my class, but this cannot be the same John Roberts. The information in this file is a mishmash of different people. I'm not sure any of them truly exist. Somebody is trying to pull something here, and I want to know why."

"So, what are you asking of me, Rachel?"

"Tell your father I'll be visiting him very shortly. I want to know where this file originated. Who dared to make this stuff up?"

"Did you want something to eat, Jon?"

A waitress came by and took Jon's order. The conversation turned to Mt. Valle and where different friends were now. Rachel told Jon I had gone to New Hampshire also, as Howard Reynolds and Art Williams did. Jon's ears perked when he heard Art Williams' name.

Rachel noticed, "Do you know Art Williams, Jon?"

"Not personally, but I have heard the Senator speak of him."

She wondered why Florin would want to speak to Williams. The two were not best buddies at Mt. Valle. She said nothing to Jon but wondered, too, how Florin knew Tippy Adams, Jonathan's father?

Tippy was supposed to be undercover. After lunch, they headed back to their jobs. Rachel stopped to get the afternoon Journal. On the front page was the picture of a protester in front of the Capitol Building in Washington, D.C. She recognized the face as that of John 'Jack Rabbit' Roberts. Rachel blew a sigh of relief.

"Well, Jack Roberts, my old friend. I know where you are now. Stay out of trouble, Jack," she said to herself. Then she noticed what he was wearing. There was something written on the front of his T-shirt,

"Let the Dominoes Fall." Jack turned around, and Rachel noticed dominoes falling over on the back of the shirt.

"Interesting shirt, Jack. Is that Florin's campaign slogan? Catchy! That must follow the bullshit rhetoric you're passing out. Don't get too crazy, Thom."

CHAPTER 8

1ˢᵗ Hearing, Court House

Abright, warm morning greeted me on my way south to Providence. Coming off the Bay, a light, cool breeze led me into the Courthouse parking lot. My father asked me to come down and sit in on a hearing for a John Roberts who had recently escaped from a Canadian prison. Dad thought a deportation order would be his argument this morning, but it wasn't. Roberts' escape was not the first thing on the list. It was a charge of murder and robbery of an elderly veteran, stealing a car, and crossing state lines. I've heard dad present cases before, but this was going to be different. The deportation request should have been on the docket.

Between cases, my mind drifted home to Howard Reynolds and his wife's unexpected demise. Because Howie was a fellow graduate of Mt. Valle, I felt especially obliged to find out who killed her. Being Police Chief at Lakes Crossing made me responsible for the town. Could I pick up any pointers here, listening to dad? I didn't know, but I was going to pay close attention.

"Your Honor, if it please the court. My client is asking that his case remain here, in Providence. The Defense recognizes the Canadian Government's want for a quick turnaround of their prisoner and the

State of New York to address and clear up the Watertown incident there. But my client is not stating he is innocent of assaulting the gentleman...." Dad was interrupted by Judge Connors.

"Let's state the charges correctly, Mr. Smalley. It's not that your client assaulted the gentleman in Watertown, New York. The man died. It is now a murder charge. Please correct your statement."

"Yes, your honor." There was a long pause before dad could figure out what to say. Judge Connors asked,

"Is there anything else, Mr. Smalley? I still need a plea. How does your client plea?"

"On which charge, your honor?" dad asked.

"Alright, if you're feeling befuddled. How about the murder charge?"

"Not guilty, your honor."

"Ok, not guilty. I won't consider the auto theft and the escape from Canada; I will let the Federal Authorities deal with those. Does the prosecution have any objections?"

"I have another request, your honor?"

Dad asked. "I will entertain one more, Mr. Smalley. What is it?"

George Trainer, the State's Chief Prosecutor, interjected,

"The State objects, your honor. We find this highly irregular. I submit the Defense is unprepared and is seeking a delay or extension of his case."

"Mr. Smalley, are you up to something? Let me caution you, sir. I am very familiar with your antics."

"Yes, your honor, and no, no antics. The Defense is requesting extra security for my client. It is believed there may be an attempt on his life."

Mr. Trainer jumps up, "I object, your honor."

Judge Connor asked my father,

"Do you have any evidence of these assertions, or allegations, or whatever you have?"

"Not yet, your honor. This information just came to my attention as we were entering the courthouse."

"How convenient." The judge looked at dad with a not-so-convincing expression on his face. The State jumped up again when the judge said,

"I know, Mr. Trainer. The State objects. I understand, but I am going to give Mr. Smalley this weekend to prepare for Monday and present the evidence of these attempts on Mr. Roberts' life". Judge Connors looked at dad and told them,

"You have this weekend only, Mr. Smalley, and this weekend only. After which, I will be holding you in contempt. You are forewarned.

"Yes, your honor, I understand."

The judge thought for a moment then asked the Prosecution, "Does the State have any objections?"

"The State finds it somewhat irregular, your Honor, but the Prosecution does not object."

Dad looked at his client, then looked at me and smiled. The judge looked at his calendar and told dad,

"Because of the holiday weekend, Court will resume on Tuesday, the 5th. I expect to see you both back in court on Tuesday morning, prepared."

The gavel fell, and the judge said, "Court is adjourned. Enjoy the Fourth, gentlemen."

"Thank you, your Honor, you also," my father replied.

"What do you have up your sleeve, Ralph?" asked the Prosecution.

"I need time, George. How can I prepare a defense when they hand it to me as I'm walking in?"

"Oh, enjoy the Fourth, George."

"You, too, Ralph," George said. George Trainer, Chief Prosecutor for the State, went head-to-head with Ralph Smalley a couple of times. Afterward, as usual, you would find them at the Lucky Duck and getting shit-faced together. Roberts turned and smiled, thanking my father for his attempt. The Sheriff took Roberts back to Wyatt while I met dad at the desk.

"Dad? What was that all about? You don't need a delay. To do what? It all looks like a slam dunk to me." I told him. And something about an attempt on Roberts' life? Is that true?" I asked.

"Hello, son. Glad you made it. You heard all that, huh?" he asked, stuffing his valise. "Come on, I'll tell you at lunch."

We rushed down to the tavern and took a table in the corner. Dad had his usual with a large order of French fries while waiting for me. After rushing to keep up with him, I begged,

"Dad, slow down!" I told him.

"Have a seat, son. What are you drinking?" dad asked. My mind was racing, and I didn't have time to think of anything.

"A beer."

Taking a breath, "Now, why are you all excited? How is a delay or extension going to help Roberts?"

"Yes." He said, briefly, "Helping Roberts."

"Okay," I asked him, "So what do you expect to get from a delay?"

"Time. I just want the time to study this thing a little more. I can see, quite plainly, Roberts is guilty, and his file says he has been guilty all his life. But why? So, I am going to find out. That is why the delay, that's why I'm the lawyer, and you're the cop."

A customer at the bar pointed to the television.

"Attorney General Albert Howe was found murdered this morning while hunting on a remote hilltop in eastern New York. Security personnel traveling with the Attorney General found he had been shot by someone using a bow and arrow. A witness reports seeing the Attorney General and his party entering the woods, but no one else was trailing after them. A team of investigators is on the scene. Stay tuned for more."

"Dad, that's the third Cabinet member assassinated in less than a month. What's going on?" I asked.

"Somebody is whittling away at the cream of Comstock's crop. How many more will be killed is anybody's guess. I suspect it will depend on what Washington does. The object lesson here is trying to get the President to quit. But that's just my guess." Dad said.

"I have to admit Comstock hasn't been the best we've had in the White House, but this is one hell of a way to make a change," I added.

I could almost feel what my father was thinking. He thought someone from high up was behind it all.

"Who would know which members to hit and where they would be?"

He looked at me and almost whispered,

"Someone with an ambition to run for President."

I did not want to touch that line other than think it could be a Rhode Island State Senator.

CHAPTER 9

The Shot-July 4

As soon as the bullets left the barrels, two bodies fell on the steps of Providence City Hall. The radios in the shooter's ears crackled open with one question,

"What color is the target?" asked the voice.

"You're the one in front of City Hall, dumb ass. You saw them fall. You tell me!"

Art ripped the walkie-talkie off his head and smashed it on the floor. There was no time for pleasantries, and the two shooters immediately went into escape mode. Art had to get out of that office before the State Police helicopter was over his position.

He quickly took down the Remington 700; barrel, receiver, suppressor and stuffed them into the duffle. The custom-made scope he tucked into the outside pocket. Now, pull off the black nylon shirt to a dirty brown 'T-shirt underneath. The dark navy slacks slide off, revealing a pair of torn and stained blue jean shorts.

Meanwhile, a young woman dressed in a custodial uniform walks hurriedly out of the Fleet Bank and down the alleyway to Westminster Street. Her backpack concealing a Remington sniper rifle. She finds her 10year old pick-up truck baking in the blazing sun. Stripping off the uniform reveals a loose-fitting blouse and a pair of Tommy Bahama shorts. She then exchanges her work shoes for the Birkenstocks kept under the seat. One turn of the ignition won't start the engine. "Not now, Mr. Ford, not now!" she tells herself. Another turn of the key, and the truck roars to life. She rolls down the windows, catching the breeze coming across the parking lot, and heads for 95 and home.

Art threw the duffle across his back, descending the ten flights of stairs, three steps at a time. The last step takes him out the side door with 25 yards to go. His car is parked on the other side of the canal at a construction site off Steeple Street. The water isn't deep but refreshing in the heat. He just can't stay to enjoy it. After a short swim, he uses the eastern bank to cover his exit from the canal. He ducks behind an old pickup and takes off the wet T-shirt, throwing it over his shoulder. The ragged top of the Volkswagen isn't going to give him any relief from the July sun, so he folds it down and stashes the duffle in the compartment behind the rear seat. Timing the State Police helicopter's coming and going over his position, he senses everything is taking longer than he planned. The police are growing curious and beginning to move in his direction. He knows he must be as far away as possible before they stop him. Jumping in the car, he turns the key, and the Bug chugs its way up Canal Street trailing clouds of white exhaust smoke. Just north of the parking lot, Police stop him.

"Was I speeding, officer?" Art surveyed both officers. "License and registration, sir." They ask."Sure." He handed over his license and registration."Shut the car off, sir," the officer told him. Art turned the car off, but the V.W. kept sputtering, choking white smoke at the officers."Can't you shut this thing off?" one said."Yeah, but it takes a minute." Suddenly the car stopped. Art looked at the two officers, shrugged his shoulders, and smiled.

One officer asked, "Does it do that all the time?"

"Uh, no, just sometimes. It is a classic. What do you expect?"

"Yeah, I know. Where are you coming from?" one officer asks.

"Book store," pointing behind him.

The officer notices two books on the passenger's seat. "*Ulysses* and *Bill the Cat?*"

The officer grinned at Art.

Art told him, "One is mine. The other is a gift. Guess which is which?"

The second officer asks, "Where are you going?"

"Home."

"And home is where?" the officer asks.

"It says it on my license, Attleboro."

"Your plate says Rhode Island."

"I just moved in with my girlfriend. I'm changing my registration over on Monday."

"You want to think about getting that smoke problem fixed, also. There is a law about that."

"Yeah. I know. I have an appointment to get that fixed on Monday, too. I just hope it's not too expensive."

"Did you see or hear anything unusual coming off the Mall?" the policeman asks.

"I'm sorry, officer, I'm not a crowd person. Since returning from Nam, I don't do well in crowds. It's too much noise, and I thought I heard a gunshot, too. No. Not for me."

"That was a firecracker," the officer says.

The second officer asks, "What outfit were you with?"

"82nd." Art says, exposing his tattoo.

The officers nodded their headsin approval and said, "Glad you made it back."

"Me, too, but I have my days," Art said, thinking, *"and this might be one of them."*

The officer handed back Art's license and registration, "Have a good day. Happy 4th."

Art pulled away, leaving the officers in a cloud of white smoke. As soon as they were out of sight, he reached under the dash and turned a small switch to bring the engine back to its proper mixture, reducing the smoke. Then he headed for I-95 North and home. He knew the black Ford pick-up in front of him. It led him into Lakes Crossing, where he watched it turn off into a new cul-de-sac.

Art pulled onto Upton Road and saw a Lakes Crossing Police cruiser pass by, heading for town. He wondered where it had come from. Driving home, he thought, *"There's not much up this way, and it takes a while to get anywhere."* He cautiously pulled into his driveway, watching for any signs of disturbance around the property. A man in dirty shorts, a t-shirt, and a Yankees ball cap was walking on the Upton Road.

"Must be a summer tourist. Yankees! Bad choice all the way around." He could see Mutts standing on the sofa back, barking up a storm, anticipating his master's return.

Backing the Volkswagen around the house, he grabbed the duffel from behind the seat, covered the car with a tarp, and entered through the back door. He walked into the living room, closed the drapes on the picture window, then sat down to clean his rifle.

CHAPTER 10

Call To Arms

S enator Thomas Florin enjoyed his bourbon at the Crosshairs Outdoor Sportsmen's Club.

"These hoodlums, these thugs; these cheap 3-piece suit mobsters," he hesitated. *"Some are members of our House and Senate in Washington, D.C., and they need to be stopped,"* he would tell them.

Few club members paid any attention to the ranting, but others found the diatribe interesting. They didn't object to his politics, only his volume.

"Not a bad speech. He's a politician for sure. Glad he's not running the country," some said.

Word spread that the club was looking for individuals with a high degree of marksmanship, those qualified to begin a 'Justice Temple.' Some members were suspicious of a 'secret side' to the Club getting started. They and the public thought the Club's purpose was just for sport, where wives were happy to send their husbands out to a place where they could enjoy their shooting hobby. They could compete, win, and return home with a trophy. But when asked to participate using 'live' targets, questions began popping up from all the members, and they started backing out.

"Rats in the building are one thing," they said. "But this sounds like you're suggesting something a lot bigger."

Three members of the Club were former Marines, and they liked the idea of live targets. After hearing the plan, they raised their hands to join this new 'Justice Temple.' Taken aside, they were asked to swear to what they were about to hear and do. They were duped into a commitment, promised to "protect and defend," as the Senator kept telling them.

"The law is being subverted, gentlemen. Twisted, to serve the certain few," he told them. *"Criminals are going free. They spit on and burn the flag. Are they Patriots? And they're being treated like children with no more than a spanking and then let go. This travesty cannot be allowed to continue. If the perpetrators cannot be brought to justice, then those that would enable such crimes to stand will be. They cannot be allowed to get away with this insult to our country."*

The three Marines looked at one another and acknowledged they understood the rules and severity of their participation. They accepted the consequences if their targets got away without punishment. To the Marines, the Senator made things 'official'. Not all the members understood. The three left for the range to sharpen their skills. The next meeting of the Justice Temple would point out a target.

"Remember, people. You swore an oath to this Temple. There is a job, not for us, but this country. We are Patriots, one and all. We love our country. Should any of you choose to relinquish membership, do it now; "say yee so, or say yee no."

Those members stepped forward. They walked over to the secretary, who handed them a non-discloser agreement. Each man signed the paper, walked out the back door, and told never to return.

The Senator now had a committed force of men and women who understood the solemn duty to meet out justice, of "being a Patriot, like me." But which shooter would get the first job? And which target would make the most significant impact on the President of the United States?

"Danger comes with each mission, ladies and gentlemen. There's no guaranty you will make it back safely. It could be in cuffs.

It could be in a body bag. Just remember why you are on that mission. Your assignments are coming, so stay sharp."

One member asked, "Was the killing of Attorney General Howe an example of meeting out justice? Is that what we are supposed to do?"

Florin paused to think of an answer reinforcing his reasoning for duping these people into signing up blindly.

"Think of who the Attorney General was working for and what the government is doing to the people. He wasn't working for me." pointing to himself.

"He wasn't working for you." Pointing to one of the Marines.

"He was working for Comstock. Ask yourself, were they helping this country or hurting it; economically, politically. You don't have to look far for a reason to clench your fists and want to strike out. Go out there, listen to the people, hear their grievances, and then come back and tell me you don't want to do something? Then you will know what the Justice Temple is all about. Someone will make the necessary changes. We are just going to push them along."

Dismissing the volunteers, he tells them,

"Now, go out there and prepare yourselves for what you have to do."

CHAPTER 11

Domino #1

It is an uncomfortably cold Monday morning on the Virginia estate of Senator Archibald Conklin, the Republican leader of the Senate. He is preparing to make his way to Washington, DC, to brief the President. The latest plan for dealing with the Native American uprising in Nebraska and the Dakotas is on the docket. The Sioux want their land back, and Archie tells them, "Like hell," in lockstep with his boss. They need help living on the reservations; medical care, schools, 'a chance!' is still their cry, after almost 200 years of the Federal thumb on their heads.

Every morning Conklin likes to impress himself by appearing in the full-length antique mirror in his study. *"If you look good in front of your constituents, they'll believe anything you tell them."* It's 6:30 AM.

"You picked out a beautiful suit, Morris," he whispers to himself, thanking his haberdasher, Morris Pickens. "This suit fits ...." The Senator jerks and grabs the frame of the mirror. He looks down and sees the front of his shirt has gone from white to bright red. The mirror has a hole and a red stain running down the length and through the glass.

The Senator turned away from the mirror, feeling the cold breeze coming through the hole cut in the window's glass. There's a face in the window, but he won't be able to tell whose face it is. Conklin falls face down, dead, on the carpet as the door to the Rose Garden slams closed.

The limousine parked in front of Conklin's home is waiting to take him to Washington, D.C. It's kept running to stay warm for the Senator when he is ready to leave. The driver has crushed out two cigarettes and is prepared to light up a third when he looks at his watch for the umpteenth time, wondering if he'll be able to leave by 08:10 AM to meet President Comstock on time. He is a stickler for punctuality. The driver wonders, *'How much faster will I have to drive to make it on time?'*

'This is most unusual,' he tells himself. *'What is keeping you, Senator?'* He shouts, turning toward the house, exits the car, and goes to the door.

Knocking on the heavy oak front door, the butler greets him and ushers the driver into the study, where they find the body of Senator Archie Conklin releasing his life's blood on the 17th century rose ladened carpet. They find a bullet hole in his chest and feel a cold breeze coming from a hole cut in the window.

"Don't touch him," the driver says as he alerts the Secret Service. The butler checks for a pulse.

"He's dead," the butler says. In minutes, the area is swarming with Secret Service. An ambulance is called, and the coroner rushes inside.

"Anybody touch the body?" he asks.

"Only to check for a pulse," the butler replies.

"You didn't turn him over?" the coroner asks again. "Hm," the coroner says. "He was shot with a large caliber weapon, possibly a .45."

He turns the body over and sees that the bullet has passed through the senator. A domino, tinged with blood, is sticking out from the Senator's breast pocket. The coroner removes the domino and finds a piece of paper attached and a partial fingerprint on the domino. Placing it in a clear evidence bag, he reads the note attached.

"#2 Mr. President. Your turn is coming."

Forensics bags the note and domino as evidence.

On the ground, outside the east window, they find the Marine, waking. A head wound reveals he was clubbed from behind. Secret Service notices the Marine's sidearm and radio are missing. They ask, "What are you doing here?"

"I was posted here as a guard for the Senator."

"Your sidearm and radio are missing," the agent says.

"I know I had them when I started."

An EMT leads the Marine to the ambulance and tends to his injury. He is taken to the hospital for observation and further questioning.

Footprints from the east window lead to the house next door. The house appears empty, but they go in to investigate. Entering the garage, they find a stool in the middle of the floor. "This looks a bit out of place, do you think?" One agent asks.

"A radio and a handgun, just sitting here?"

Forensics bags the weapon, "It's a Glock-47." They find the rest of the house is locked and secured then return to the Senator's home. An agent finds the blood-stained mirror has a hole, chest high, going through it.

"He must have been standing in front of the mirror when shot." The agent finds a hole in the wall behind the mirror. He pulls out his pocket knife and removes a bullet. "Looks like a 45," he concludes. Now, they have to match the bullet to a weapon.

"The weapon in the garage is a Glock-47, a 9mil. No match there. Bag 'em, let Forensics figure it out."

A second agent finds a glass cutting tool on the ground where the Marine was found.

"Why would the gunman leave this behind? Did he drop it or discard it?" They bag the cutter and search for more evidence. Footprints leading in and out of the study go through the rose garden and into a wooded grove, disappearing into the neighborhood next door. They find a red Fiat Spyder parked and locked.

"Neighbor's car?" the lead agent asks. "Canvas the neighborhood, find out who the car belongs to."

At the hospital, an F.B.I. agent questions the Marine about what happened before the shooting.

"I didn't know I had duty for the Senator until the night before. He had asked for a Marine Guard, and I was picked. I've had D.C. duty in the past, but not for a Senator. I was told to carry my sidearm; they gave me the radio, and I was assigned to the east side of the mansion. I stood outside the East window and found it closed and locked when I got there. My back was to the window so I couldn't see anything inside. I was listening to the senator's music when I heard something. I turned to investigate, and the lights went out. That's it."

The agent told him,

"We found your sidearm. A .45, right?"

"No, I carry a Glock 47. I don't know where that came from." The Marine tells him.

"Well, somebody put a .45 through the senator's chest, and we have to find the bullet and the gun."

The doctor reported the Marine should stay the night so nurses could watch him for any adverse effects of the clubbing. If he sleeps the whole night, he may go home in the morning.

"You received a pretty good whack on the head, Marine," the doctor tells him. "We will probably let you go home in the morning. How far is home?"

"Rhode Island," the Marine tells him.

"That's a-ways," an agent says. "By the way, we found your Glock 47 in the house next door."

"Can I get it back?" The Marine asks.

"When Forensics is done with it, you'll get it back." the agent tells him. The doctor instructs the Marine,

"I'll be here in the morning to make sure you're fit to travel. Don't leave before you see me. Alright?"

"I'll wait for you, doc. Thanks," the Marine answers. In the morning, the doctor okay's the Marine to leave the hospital. He hails a cab to take him out to the Senator's neighborhood. His red Fiat Spyder is still there, locked and waiting for him. Setting his GPS for home, he travels around the Beltway and heads north. Turning on the radio, he hears,

> ***"In this morning's headlines, Republican Senate Leader Archibald Conklin, President Comstock's right-hand man, was assassinated this morning at his estate in Virginia. The Senator was scheduled to meet with the President to discuss the latest uprisings on the Sioux Reservation. Secretary of the Interior, Robert White Feather, has been fighting to clarify the new provisions of the comprehensive treaty. Those provisions gave all governing tribal bodies complete autonomy within the Reservations' borders in all contiguous 48 States. Republican opposition has stalled the implementation of those provisions and the signing of the agreement."***
>
> ***The investigation into Senator Conklin's death continues."***

President Comstock was called about the Senator's death just as it hit the morning news.

"Someone got to Conklin," the President tells V-P James Holloway. "Anyone know who might have done this, any idea? We were going to discuss the Indian thing."

"Wait, that's the Native American Agreement, I believe you're referring to, Mr. President," Holloway emphasizes.

Conklin glares at Holloway, "Do you suppose it was one of them? Those ungrateful sons-of-bitches! And what happened to that Marine Guard he specifically asked for?"

"We are working on it, Mr. President," Alex Vaines, Director of the FBI, says.

"Well, work a little harder, damn it. This thing will be cold, and the killer gone before noon if he's not gone already."

An agent gives Director Vaines the note. He reads it then hands it to the President.

"We will have to put you under tighter security, sir."

"Bullshit!" Comstock declares. "I wear a vest now. I will continue to wear it. You just do your job."

"Yes, Sir," Vaines answered.

Roadblocks are set up for 20 miles in all directions, stopping and searching all vehicles. They were looking for someone with a gun in the car, specifically a 45 cal.

Back in Providence, Senator Florin gets a phone call.

"Mission complete, sir," the Marine tells him. "Thank you for the opportunity to serve my country again."

That call put a smile on the Senator's face. Now he feels the implementation of the Justice Temple was going to bear fruit, but he had to see what President Comstock was going to do. How he answered the killing was not going to be with the law; the FBI and Secret Service would do that. The Senator wanted to see what changes Comstock would make in his governance. No changes would mean another Marine was going after another member of Congress.

Florin wanted to ask the Marine how he pulled the job off when he got back at the Club. Late that afternoon, a red Fiat pulled into the parking lot. The Marine made his way in and saw the Senator in the doorway.

"Good afternoon, Marine." It was the Senator.

"Good afternoon, sir," the Marine answers.

"I take it everything went well, no hang-ups?"Florin asks.

"No hang-ups, sir."

"You'll have to tell me how you pulled it off," Florin continues to question the Marine.

"I can't do that, sir. It would be a breach of protocol. The secrets of any operation are to be kept as secrets. You said as much yourself, sir. If we tell, we break security." The Marine explains.

"I know you understand, sir."

"Oh, yes, of course. I did say that, didn't I." Florin concedes, watching the Marine in his discipline. He notices the Marine doesn't have the .45. "You're missing your sidearm, Marine."

"Yes, sir. The FBI has it. I wore gloves, sir. They won't find any fingerprints."

"I hope not. I don't want this coming back to me, you understand?" Florin barks.

"Yes, sir," the Marine answered.

A week later, members noticed the Marine failing to attend any further meetings of the Justice Temple. After inquiries were made, the Senator's response was,

"We all have personal business at home that needs to be taken care of, ladies and gentlemen. He'll show up."

A week later, State Police find a red Fiat Spyder abandoned in the parking lot at Lincon Woods. They find bloodstains on the seat and headrest. Forensics finds a receipt for a toll along the New Jersey Turnpike, dated one week ago, the day of Senator Conklin's murder. Captain January is wondering if there is a connection. While examining the GPS, he finds the car and possibly the Marine was in Virginia the same day the Senator was assassinated.

Director Vaines orders an agent to determine who owns the Fiat Spyder to ensure it isn't involved in the Senators murder. He suspects it might belong to the Marine.

CHAPTER 12

The Crosshairs-Second Visit

Cpt. January,

"…the short drive to the club gave me time to think. Who do I speak with when I got there? A backyard Zamboni was cleaning the parking lot when I arrived. A wonderfully cut front fascia greeted me as I reached for the heavy wooden door. An ominous giant bullseye was carved into the face of it. Inviting and suggestively exotic. Maybe they go on safaris, I thought. Pulling open one of the doors, I walk in to find a young man standing at a welcome desk. I paused, thinking, this guy looks familiar.

"Jonathan?"

He looked up and smiled, *"Captain Homer January! What are you doing here? Need some practice? The range is open."*

"No, Jon, thanks, I'm accurate. I didn't know you were a gun guy. How long have you been coming here?

"Almost four years. Yeah, four years. My college had a shooting club. I thought I'd see what it was about, so I joined. I've been having a good time ever since. I even went so far as to buy myself a target rifle and a handgun. They're only 22's, but I don't need anything bigger than that for target shooting."

Suddenly, a bell went off in my head. He's got a rifle and a pistol, and they're both 22's.

"*So,*" Jon asks, "*What brings you here?*"

"*I'm in the middle of an investigation, and I found my deceased victims were all members here. Can you tell me anything of what you do here?*" I asked. "*But first, can you give me the name of the president of this club?*" I asked.

"*Tom,*" Jon told me.

"*Just Tom? Does he have a last name?*"

"*We don't use last names here, Homer. It's a rule that members must use first names only. It fosters conversation, though I will say the shooters here concentrate more on their score than on casual conversation.*"

"*No last names? You need one to sign your paycheck.*" Homer insisted.

"*And I use my last name when I sign my paycheck. But…*"

It was no more than casual conversation since we off-handedly knew one another. Jon's regular job was secretary to Senator Thomas Florin. I would see him there whenever I had business in the Capital. I looked at him, wondering why he was so reluctant to talk to me about the Club.

"*What are you worried about, Jon?*" I asked. He motioned to me to follow him out to the parking lot so that we could talk away from prying eyes and ears. Several times he turned around to see who might be watching. Except for the guy on the Zamboni, there were only three cars in the lot. The one belonging to the guy driving the Zamboni, Jon's, and mine.

"*There's no one here but you and I, Jon.*" We stopped between cars, and I asked,

"*Give me a break, will ya. This is a shooting club, right?*" My questioning was stern and direct.

"*Yes,*" he answered. "*Yes, it is. But membership has a vow of confidentiality. We are not supposed to be talking to the police.*" Jon was far from calm and collected.

"*Why not? What have you got to hide here? Are you doing something illegal? Don't your members come here to have a good time, prac-*"

tice their shooting skills, have a drink, and shoot the bull? It sounds like your president is worried about something."

I forced my questions, trying to shake the tree. Something had to fall out that would connect the deaths of the three Marines. I spotted a second door, a few feet away from the main entrance.

"That other door, next to the entrance, where does it lead?

"To a small meeting room used by the Justice Temple," he said.

"Justice Temple? What is that, some kind of legal thing?" I pushed.

"No. It's a separate club for exceptional shooters."

"Exceptional shooters? What do they do?" I kept pushing him. I could see he had answers but was reluctant to talk.

"I've said enough already," He said, then paused before telling me, *"I have to go back inside. I've been out here too long. If you want more, you will have to get a warrant."*

"Jonathan, wait a minute. Okay, I'll get a warrant." I told him. *"But I have to ask you…."* I pulled out the photo. *"Do you know these men?"*

He turned to look at the picture. I watched the color wash from his face.

"Yes. I do; they are all members here, great shooters, all of them." He answered like he was kicking a can down the road with his hands in his pockets.

"They were, Jon. They're all dead, murdered, execution-style. This fourth guy, I don't know if he's dead or alive. I don't even know his name, but I have to find him if he's to stay alive. Do you know who he is, Jon?" I wasn't going to let up on him even though we knew one another.

"Don't tell me you're part of any wrongdoing, Jon. Rachel would not like to hear that." He looked at me with surprise. I told him, *"Yes, I know that you see Rachel occasionally, and I don't care what kind of relationship you're sharing with her. But I have got to find out who killed these men and why. If you know something, anything, Jon, you've got to tell me."* He took a deep breath and finished saying, *"Get a court order,"* then went back inside.

"God ..." I left, swearing inside, "more damn work to do." I drove back to the station, not feeling especially satisfied. Homer knew Jon was restrained by the club's rules but thought Jon had the answers to questions he would ask. "If I get a court order, would he talk to me? Would we still be friends?"

CHAPTER 13

New Duties-Lakes Crossing

My day was going along smoothly. Buster and I Inspected the office and made the changes we needed to make it easier to work. I knew the names of my attentive Corporal-receptionist and the Captain from the States Forensics team. It would take me a while to learn the other characters' names on my Roto-Desk. I had to find out how important they would be. I put together a short litany of yesterday's happenings and what I had to deal with today.

All the cells are empty. Howard Reynolds is having breakfast in his own home. He saw the judge yesterday, and Lawyer Jeffrey Bowes made his bail. Great. Reynolds' wife is still lying on a slab in the morgue, and I have to find her murderer. I knew it wasn't the fall down the stairs that killed her; the Medical Examiner said so. But who administered the sedative that did kill her? I had some work ahead of me.

My inauguration day, I call it, turned out to be a long welcome. But everything was put aside for today so that I could spend time with the office books. I needed to find out how much the Town and the State contributed to keeping Lakes Crossing alive and running.

I'm no whiz at finances, but judging by the signature on the bottom of the page, somebody in town is.

"Hey, Billie?" I yelled out. Billie came running. "Does Lakes Crossing have a CPA?"

"Well, we used to. Marjorie died three months ago."

"Now, why did she do that? Just when I needed to ask questions."

"She was 97 years old, Boss. It was her time."

"Not on my calendar," I sighed. "I guess I'll have to find a new one. Do you know anyone in town that knows Accounting, Billie?"

"I'll look that up, Boss, and have an answer for you."

I made the best of the department's books with my limited knowledge of Finances. I kept coming up with a lucrative bottom line. What I saw made me think of getting an office secretary so Billie could go out and do his job. As Chief, I would have other duties to keep me busy, even in this small town.

Billie and I shared the phone duties with the contacts he had. Several ladies and one gentleman came in applying for the job. They each had a CPA business, all very successful, judging by their dress alone. Each told their own story of working with, for, or against Marjorie, the last person to have touched the books of the Lakes Crossing Police Department. I had to respect Marjorie for her creative ideas in balancing the books. Everything looked straight and true, accurate and honest when I dove into them, but I wanted to make sure I had the cash Marjorie said I had. So, I hired the gentleman who already had a CPA business, Granite State Accounting, Certified. I would have him come in once a month to check the books and work them correctly. I found that the office never spent any money. State and Town contributions were sitting in a savings account.

After Charles Hathaway, CPA went through the books for the first time; we sat down to discuss the future fluid level of the Station. How much could I afford to spend and still keep our heads above water?

"Oh, if you wanted to hire a secretary/receptionist, go right ahead. There's enough in the account for a $30,000 a year person. It's not like the police force in Lakes Crossing is a major entity in law enforcement. There are only the two of you, and it looks like the State is supporting you quite a bit."

"Right," I said. "Well, I'll start with someone at that rate, but if the State makes changes, then I

will have to adjust according to their change."

Oh," Hathaway exclaimed. He gave a slight chuckle and said, "And that would include me."

"Well, knowing the job isn't permanent, subject to State input, I think I will tender my resignation now." He got up, shook my hand, sort of, and walked out of my office.

"I'll expect a check in the mail for my time. Thank you." And he was gone.

"$30,000 a year isn't a bad salary for the requirements of the job. I should be able to find acompetent individual to fill the position. I'll get started on that right away."

I thanked Charles Hathaway just as he closed the door. "I hope he heard me."

Hathaway was backing his $60,000 Tesla out just as I got to the door. "That thing is so quiet, so sleek, so nose-in-the-air." Then I looked at my pickup. *'Yeah, I can still kick his ass.'* I thought.

I composed an ad and sent several copies to the Concord Monitor and the Manchester Union Leader. They helped me place an ad that would guarantee results. It worked. I got results within the first week, with twelve resumes. I sent out *"Sorry, but…"* letters to those wanting to negotiate a larger top salary limit. Others wanted to know how busy the office was. When I called to tell them about the office, they laughed at Lakes Crossing having only two officers.

"Thank you, but no thank you," is what I heard before they hung up. Maybe they thought they'd be bored to death, so I scratched them off the list. The last applicant was a high school math whiz, a senior living on the outskirts of town. Eighteen and very pretty, I could see her glasses were taking something away from her appearance. She told me she tried contact lenses, but they irritated her eyes and gave her a headache. The glasses she wore were the only ones her parents could afford. I asked her,

"Do they do the job you want them to do? Is the prescription correct?"

"Yes, I think so. The doctor in Concord tested my eyes and said these should do the trick. That's how he put it."

"Ok," I said. "I would like you to look at these books and tell me what you see." It took her a couple of minutes to scan the entries.

"The bottom lines are different in both, and they should be the same." She showed me the errors and how they might have occurred. And after I had hired a CPA to check my books. Elizabeth Knowles spent all of two minutes, maybe less. I timed her. I made a point of post scripting Mr. Charles Hathaway when I sent the final check to close out his employ. I was glad he 'tended' his resignation, as he put it.

Elizabeth lived outside of Lakes Crossing with her parents and three brothers. She was the oldest, "and the smartest," she proudly said. Her mother was a work-at-home mom with her own baking business.

"What does she bake?" I asked.

"Cookies, bread, fruit pies, when the fruit are in season. On special occasions, a wedding cake."

"Do you help in the kitchen?"

"Oh, yeah, especially with the cookies. I like thinking up different kinds, and they sell pretty well. It's fun. Mom says of those; I get 50% of the profit. It's not much, but it adds up."

I was having fun talking with her. She was imposing, bright; I placed her on a level above me. I decided to hire her after showing me the finance errors. When she told me her mom made fresh bread, that cliched it. I asked what her father did for a living. She asked if I knew the name, Knowles & Barker.

"Yes, I do. They make quality stationery products. I have a couple of their pens." I told her.

"Oh, that's nice. Some of the finest writing instruments in the world my father designed, and his partner, Barton Barker, made them."

"And you father's first name," I asked.

"Robert, Robert Knowles. A couple of years ago, there was a downturn in the market. The computer reduced the need for anyone to carry a quality pen or even a good pencil. The market calls for cheap pens and pencils. Dad gets excited when an order comes in for a high line pen, one he has to design for someone special. He tells mom, "*I can buy an extra can of soup this week.*" Things aren't that bad. Dad likes to kid, wishing he could do more for us. Mom doesn't worry, though. She jokes back by telling him not to worry, "but, Robert, we're always rolling in dough." I think dad kindly laughs at mom's jokes, even though he's heard them before."

"So, that's your family. And your brothers are, brothers. They're younger and mischievous, but you love them anyway. I know. I envy you and your parents, your brothers. You have each other, and that makes a nice family." I looked her in the eyes and told her,

"You're hired. When do you want to start?"

Her expression was a turn of her head and a pause, thinking of her reply. She calmly sat there, said thank you, then,

"Well, because I'm a senior and my grades are A+'s in every subject, I think I can get some split time, a few hours in the morning, and a few in the afternoon. I can stay till 6:00 PM if you need me that long, or until 5:00 so I could be home to help my mom."

"Since the week has started, can you come in tomorrow, say 8:00 AM?"

"I'll be here. Thank you again, Chief Smalley. This opportunity will help my family out a great deal."

As she was leaving, she turned around with one more question.

"My father wanted me to be sure to ask. Is there any insurance? and the benefits that come with the job?"

It was a good question. I wondered why she hadn't asked during the interview.

"You are fully covered, Elizabeth, 100%, plus dental, two weeks off the first year, and two days added every year up to a total of four weeks per calendar year. You get all federal holidays off and recognized religious observances, as they pertain to you. Coffee in the office is free, and so are the donuts, if you can get to them before Billie. If you need any help with the phone, let us know. Billie can answer almost all the hard questions. Anything else?"

"No, thank you. See you tomorrow." She was the most polite 18-year old I had ever met, and she rode a beat-up Vespa scooter to the station. I watched her put her helmet on and zip away on the little blue and white "Rocket." I had to laugh, watching her put-put down the road. The Vespa looked as if her father had rescued it from a fate of rusting degradation. Elizabeth told me his hobby was tinkering with small-engine vehicles.

I wondered, "*What does she does in the winter?*" I asked myself.

CHAPTER 14

Call It Home

Buster and I found a house on the lake. It sat empty for several months before I made an offer. The owner was willing to let it go, discounted to the new Chief of Police. The terms on both sides were agreed to, and after signing too many papers and giving the bank a significant down payment, I felt the pangs of diminished savings and the pride of owning my own home. The real estate agent gave me the keys to the front door, and the previous owner personally handed me the codes to the security system he had installed.

"A security system. Wow." I wondered what made him install a security system. Was it because of the neighborhood, the neighbors, or maybe he needed the system to protect himself from a past? It didn't matter now because the house felt right. And being a homeowner felt good, too.

The next thing was filling the house with furniture. I took a day to shop the outlets where the selection was the greatest. My new home wasn't very big, so I didn't need to spend a whole lot on fancy pieces. I was getting into the country look and liked the styles. It didn't take long to make up my mind, and the stores promised delivery in three days. I could now think about putting the sleeping bag away and the hot plate and cooking on a real stove. The satellite company had been in, the phone company, and the heating company had checked the furnace and filled the oil tank.

I had a chimney sweep come in to check out my large fireplace, and he ok'd the chimney and the hearth as safe and clean. I thought it too early, though, to go chopping wood or carrying it in the house. I just wanted to settle in first. The stove and refrigerator arrived, so Buster and I did a little grocery shopping. It wasn't difficult dropping a hundred bucks for a week's worth of groceries for a small dog and me.

When the furniture arrived, I didn't expect to see so many boxes with labels on the sides reading,

'*Assembly Instructions Inside.*' The pre-assembled tables and chairs required more tools than I had. My toolbox was left behind in Rhode Island. I did not think I would need it right away. The owner of the General Store and I became good friends as I picked up the tools I needed.

Early one morning, the sound of scratching at the back door got me up a little earlier than I had planned. Buster needed to go out to survey and mark his territory. I let him run while I brewed a pot of coffee. It was sunrise and time for me to get up anyway. The early morning air and the tranquil water across the lake left me hypnotized, standing in the doorway in my underwear. While soaking in the morning sun, I suddenly realized Buster was taking a little too long. I went to the back door and called out to him. He came trotting back, followed by another dog and its owner.

She spotted me standing there in my embarrassment and quickly turned around. I did the same, made an '*Excuse me,*' and ran to put on some pajamas.

"I'm sorry to surprise you like that," I said. "It was a warm night, and…."

"Oh, don't apologize. I sleep that way, too, some nights," She admitted.

"Hi, Lorraine Booker, your neighbor. You're the new Police Chief, aren't you?"

"Hi. Yes, Grant Smalley. I'm still getting used to the town, the people, the house."

"Oh, that won't take long. I've lived here all my life. I was born here," she bragged. "The people are friendly. Summer people tend to be more amicable than the regulars, so you won't have any trouble telling them apart."

"What's your dog's name?" she asked.

"Buster Piddle," I said. "And yours?"

"Virginia Pride," she said, "But I call her *Ginnie.* I rescued her from a shelter in Virginia when I

was on vacation last year. She came right to me, so I knew we were right together."

"Do you want to come in for coffee?" I asked. "I just put a pot on."

"Well, I'm not dressed to go visiting," she said with some embarrassment.

"Oh, I thought I took care of that earlier." I wisecracked.

"Well, alright," she said. "But just one cup. I don't want to stay long. I'm sure you have things you have to do today."

I brewed enough for a couple of cups, and I have to admit it was pretty good for my first time.

"That was the first time you've ever made coffee?" she exclaimed. "Well, it came out very well. I like it."

That sounded like a setup for more visits. We talked about the dogs and the town. She was born in Lakes Crossing but wouldn't tell me how long ago. She looked about 30, maybe 35 years old, attractive, with a shapely figure that she did not attempt to hide under her bathrobe. My father told me never to ask a woman's age, and I wasn't going against that adage.

Not long into our conversation, she began to get familiar. Her eyes grew wide, and she slowly moved closer and closer to me. I took the hint, and we ended up on the floor. It didn't matter to her how hard the floor was; she came after me just as hard. Her experience ran all over my young ass, and we both fell into the moment and enjoyed the company. After more than an hour of swapping spit, we recognized we couldn't polish the linoleum anymore. I got up first and aggressively pulled her to me. We didn't say anything that offered any future encounters. She grabbed Ginnie's leash and went home.

Buster and I jumped in the shower, and I got myself ready for work. It was now after 10:00 AM, so I called the office.

"I'm on my way in, Billie."

"Okay, boss."

Turning on the TV, I picked up on the news I hadn't seen or heard in a couple of days. The murder of Senator Archie Conklin, Leader of the Senate, was all over the tube. It happened at his home in Virginia while he was dressing for a meeting with the President. My instincts as P.I. kicked in, and I started analyzing what evidence the news was releasing. The Senator had a Marine guard? I found that unusual. Most often, it's the Secret Service.

I called a friend in D.C. who had his fingers in government wranglings. He told me a certain senator had recommended a Marine guard. I wondered who that Senator was. He must have had the power to pull back the Secret Service as well. I let it go for now and headed to the station.

I wondered how Howard and Sandy Reynolds found out about this beautiful little town or brought Art Williams up here. He has a small cabin a few miles up the western shore. It was isolated, but I chalked that up to his PTSD from Nam. I hadn't talked to him since he returned from Nam. Friends in R.I. said he *checked out.* Speaking to his parents, they told me their son disappeared, inside and out.

"He's not the same person, Grant, that graduated Mt. Valle," his dad told me.

The Reynolds purchased a lovely home on a cul de sac. It had a beautiful view of the lake and was the only house in that area, a quiet spot for writers to gather their thoughts. I guess Howard thought the laid-back lifestyle would better deal with his Nam experience. Now he was dealing with his wife's death. It's a hard thing coming to grip with the possibility that your wife, your chosen partner, may have been murdered. You're constantly asking why.

Lakes Crossing is not a heavily populated town, but it is touristy. An apartment building with twenty rooms, a small campground on the outskirts of town with forty lakeside sites for campers with vehicles, and thirty more for tents. In season, it's always packed. The two restaurants in town are kept busy and always looking for help. Smack in the middle of Main Street; the one general store has a breakfast counter serving the best coffee in town. It puts the restaurants to shame, but the convenience of being next to the police station means Billie and I get to use it often.

Buster and I habit walking to the station on good mornings. Main Street is barely crowded. One morning, I saw a little yellow Volkswagen coming through headed West. The sun, reflecting off the lake, made it difficult to see the driver or passenger, even with my sunglasses. I let it go as a tourist out for a ride. I liked taking Buster out every morning before going to the station. It means less interruption during my day, it keeps him healthy and me informed of my town's health. That sounded strange, 'My Town,' but I welcomed it. Billie was watching TV when we walked in one morning.

"Hey, Billie. What's made the news today?" I asked.

"It looks like the President lost another member of his Cabinet, boss. What's going on? Is one guy knocking off Senator after Senator, or is it a gang looking to overthrow the government?"

"It is a bit strange, I know, Billy. It's like the killer is trying to make a point, but somebody in DC

is not listening. I hope the politicians in Washington get the point before the shooter empties Congress."

CHAPTER 15

Domino #2

A ketch sets out on Keeler Bay, heading for the calm waters of Lake Champlain. US Treasury Secretary Mitchel Snipes is at the helm, while a crew of six armed guards acts like they know what they're doing on a boat. Andrea, the Secretary's wife, gets up and makes her way aft along the rail. As the ketch comes around the southern point of Kellogg Island, Snipes jerks and goes white knuckles on the wheel. His wife falls across the cabin, a bright red spot growing on her jersey. Three feet from them, a bodyguard notices the Secretary's actions, then the blood coming from his back. He calls out, "Sniper! Everybody down." He grabs Snipes' shirt pulling him to the deck. Checking both victims for a pulse, he finds none. He only sees the gaping holes of the exit wounds.

The guards drop to the deck and peel both shorelines. The shots could have come from anywhere, passing between Kellogg Island and the last point on Keeler Bay. Security on the ground moves as a helicopter is dispatched from the Air National Guard Base in Burlington, 10 minutes away. Dropping the sails, a guard motors the boat to the nearest dock. The homeowner comes out and questions why the ketch is mooring at his dock. The guard shows his badge and tells the owner,

"We have an incident here. The Secretary has been injured. You and your family need to remain in place and not get in the way. Forget what you see here. An ambulance is on the way, and there will be more activity. Please stay out of the way."

The ambulance arrives and takes the bodies of the Secretary and his wife to the nearest hospital, where they are pronounced dead. Searching the boat for clues, Forensics finds a domino under the wheel with a note tied to it. The message and the domino are presented to the FBI. The agent reads,

"#2, Mr. President. Next move is Yours."

Angrily Comstock bellows, "Another domino? What does this prick expect me to do, sit down and play a game of dominoes with him? Is that what this is all about?" He paces about the Oval Office, trying to control his rage, then sees the news of Snipes' death on the television.

"This just in… Treasury Secretary Mitchel Snipes has been assassinated this morning while sailing his ketch, the Madam Do-Bay, on Lake Champlain. The Secretary's wife, sailing with him, was also killed. Security personnel assigned to the Secretary were not injured. An investigation is underway. We'll have more as the story develops."

"And this leak! How the hell does the press have the news before I do? You find out who it is. I'll hang the bastard from the Capitol Rotunda. Now get out of here."

"Snipes," Comstock laments to Holloway, "They got Snipes and his wife. Why kill his wife? Such a nice lady." Loudly he wonders,

"And the press reports the news before I get it." Pacing the Oval Office, he bangs his fist on the desk with every pass by.

"The guards on the boat? Where were they? They didn't see or hear anything?"

"No, Mr. President," says FBI Director Vaines. "The boat was half a mile out from either shore.

There was no one in the water, no other boats, no one swimming. The shot had to come from shore and fired through a silencer."

"No one onshore, no one in the neighborhood saw or heard anything?" Comstock yells.

"The only people we encountered were those that came out to the dock, the renter and his wife.

The rest of the neighborhood, the whole of the rest of the island, was pretty dead." Vaines responded.

"Choose another word, Alex. This concerns my secretary," Comstock screams.

"I'm sorry, Mr. President," Vaines answers.

An FBI forensics team searches the area for any possible clue. They searched the house looking for a weapon, a spent shell casing, even the lingering odor of a spent round. They swept the grounds for any area a shooter could have been hiding, even the house, and they found nothing. They interview the couple renting the home, finding it was their first time in Vermont.

After three days of intensive searching, the team leaves. The couple in the house are told,

"Do not disturb anything on the premises. Another FBI team will be here for a second sweep."

After the noise on the Kibbe Farm Road quiets down, the couple prepares to leave. The man carries out the breakdown receiver of a sniper rifle wrapped in newspaper. The woman carries out a small pouch containing the scope and silencer. A hidden compartment behind the rear seat of the yellow Bug convertible hides the bundle and the scope. The two have the confidence of a successful escape.

"Florin has got to do a better job of surveilling his targets. The bastard said there would be only two guards with Snipes. Then we find six. And what the hell was that Marine doing up here? His job was to plant the note and the domino and get out. Now he's seen us."

"Well, it's done," she says. "Why don't we enjoy the ride and forget about him?"

CHAPTER 16

Checking In

Art made a call to Senator Florin's office. Jonathan answers, "Good afternoon, Senator Thomas Florin's office. This is Jonathan. How may I help you today?"

"Jon, it's Brother 1, from the club. Is the Senator in?"

"Not at the moment. I expect him this afternoon. Can I take a message?"

"Yes, please. Tell the Senator the job in Vermont went well. There were no hang-ups, and please tell him, 'Thank you,' for allowing us to serve our country again. Have a nice day." Then he hung up.

Jon didn't have time to respond, but the recorder was running. He wrote down the message and placed it on the Senator's desk. Near the noon hour, he went out to have lunch with his father, Tippy Adams.

"Hi, dad."

"Hello, son. How are things at work today?" his father asks, looking about the area.

"Things aren't bad, busy. I got a message from Rachel. She wants to see you about something." Jon told him.

"Did she say what for or when?"

"No. I guess she knows how to get hold of you besides through me." Jon is aware his dad keeps surveying the area. "Don't worry, dad. This area is good. We have Security walking the perimeter all day."

"Yeah, I know. It's just this feeling I get to be extra careful. Anyway, what did you bring me for lunch?"

"First, here is your coffee, and here's your steak and cheese sub. I only got you half because you told me you were going on a diet."

"You didn't have to listen to me, you know. Did you get any chips?"

"Yes, here's a bag for you. I took a call today from a guy calling himself Brother 1. He left a message for the Senator, saying the job in Vermont went smoothly, and wanted to thank the Senator for the chance to serve his country again. Does that sound meaningful to you?"

"Yeah, it does. If you haven't heard, Secretary Snipes and his wife were killed aboard their boat yesterday afternoon, sailing Lake Champlain in Vermont." Tippy paused in thought, then suddenly got up and left.

"Dad, where are you going?" Jon asked.

"Got to run. I just remembered something. Talk to you later, son."

Jon finished his lunch and went back to the office. He called Rachel to tell her about the call from Brother 1.

"That was this morning, Jon? Thom Florin doesn't have a brother."

"Yes, about an hour ago. I had lunch with dad, and he flew off someplace after I told him. Would you know why Rachel?"

In the middle of the conversation, Senator Florin walked in, and Jon interrupted her,

"I understand, mam. I will tell the Senator. Oh, wait, here he is now. Would you like to speak to him?"

Rachel said yes, catching Jon entirely by surprise. "Please wait. I'll connect you."

"Who is it, Jon?" Tom asks.

"Rachel Biggar."

"What the hell does she want?"

"Tickets for the Senator's State Ball." Jon laughs.

"Funny, Jon. Put her through."

"Rachel, how nice to hear from you. What brings the call?"

"Had you heard of the assassination of Secretary Snipes and his wife yesterday?" Rachel asks.

"Yes, on vacation in Vermont. Do you have any contacts in DC, Rachel, that might shed some light on all of this? First, it was Conklin, now Snipes; what's going on?" Tom's question was digging into anything Rachel's office might have.

"I thought you might know, Thom. You're more connected than me. Would you let me know if this begins to impact the State, Thom? I'd hate to see you fall victim to this mad man's rage."

"Well, thank you, Rachel. I appreciate the caring. And I will let you know if I find out anything,"

"It's politics, Thom, all politics." She hangs up.

"Bitch!" he says, slamming the phone down.

Walking into his office, he sees the messages Jon left. Noticing one came from Brother 1, Art Williams, he immediately picks up the phone and dials Brother 1.

"Hello," Art answers.

"Didn't I tell you not to call my office, Art? If either of us gets pinched, it's not a big leap from you to me. And if you do have to call, make it an emergency, for crying out loud," Thom explains. Art is silent, listening to someone who has never fired at a human target.

"Senator, slow down. I hear what you're saying, and Brother 1 is a cover. They don't know who I am," Art adds, "unless you told them, Thom."

"You dumb shit. Why would I tell them who you are?"

"I haven't figured that out yet, Thom. I called to tell you the job in Vermont went well. Sandy and I evaded the Secret Service, the FBI, and all the other security Snipes had around him. Sandy makes an excellent lookout, much better than you, Thom. Get your facts straight the next time, or you'll be doing the job yourself. And that Marine you sent to place the message and domino on the boat? He got a bit zealous, Thom. He saw us; he saw Sandy and me. You fix this, Thom. You fix it, or I will." Art slammed the phone down to let Thom know he was agitated, pissed off.

Thom slammed the receiver down and cursed Art's arrogance. "That son-of-a-bitch." Then called Jonathan.

"Jon? Would you get me a coffee, please?"

"Coming right up," Jon tells him. "Everything all right, Senator? I heard you slam the receiver down."

"Some of my constituents can really get to me, Jon. But don't worry about it. I'm ok. Just the coffee."

"Coming right up."

CHAPTER 17

Paying Respects

M y father called to tell me his longtime friend and partner, Oscar Biggar, had passed away from a massive heart
attack. Services were in two days; he asked if I could
make it.

"Yeah, I'll be there, dad. My deputy can handle it for the day."

"Okay, son. I'll see you Tuesday."

We met at the church, and I paid my respects to Oscar's widow
Elaine and Rachel. People were talking of the assassination of Senate
Leader Archie Conklin, a very prominent member of the President's
Cabinet. They were surprised to hear the shooter had gotten away and
wondered who was going to pull President Comstock's strings now?

To hear Secretary Snipes and his wife were both assassinated
made people nervous. Some people at the funeral were highly connected, fearing they could be next, but no one thought the killer
could be standing right beside them. There had been no communication from him or them.

I asked dad about it.

He said, "Let's get drunk. The Lucky Duck isn't far," He added.

"Wait, dad. We can't just leave and not go to the reception. People will expect to see you there. You were partners, after all. For how many years, dad?"

"More than 40 years, son; more than 40 years," he said in reflection.

"I'll buy the drinks this time, dad."

Rachel was accepting condolences from old friends of Oscar. Lawyers from other firms were in attendance, and several State Reps and Congressmen. Dad introduced me to the bar with a beer while he grabbed a scotch and soda. I grabbed an extra beer and headed over to see Rachel. "Excuse me, pop."

"Rachel," I offered the beer and then my hand in sympathy, "Again, I'm sorry about Oscar. He was a good man. I liked him."

"Thank you, Grant. He was a good man," she paused, then asked, "And how are things in New Hampshire?"

"Things are good. I had forgotten to thank you for your kind words to my A.G. I appreciate you thinking so highly of me, Rachel." Her smile was award-winning. "I'm still getting used to the office, the personnel. The State is beautiful; a view of the lake out the living room window, which the dog loves, and I like the town. It's small but complete. I don't know the people yet, but I'm getting there."

"I had a feeling you would enjoy it up there after talking with the Attorney General. He was very cordial but with a funny accent." She went on warmly,

"You know, I was concerned when you left my party that night of the accident. I thought you had gone with John and Eddy. I saw them ask if you wanted a ride, but I didn't see you refuse to go. I was glad you didn't."

Surprised to hear that, I searched for anything to fill the conversation.

"Yeah. I felt bad about that. It seems so long ago. That night was the first time I met Homer January. We became friends after he gave me a ride home."

We both smiled while going back through the memories. It was difficult for me not to stare into those deep blue eyes. We walked over to the bar to see dad when I asked about the assassination of Archie Conklin. She took a sip of the beer and said,

"It was a shock when I heard it this morning. It will be challenging for the Senate to hold its place against the House. And President Comstock will have to find another henchman to do his bidding in the Senate. Now, the Snipes killing, and his wife. Why kill his wife?" It was a puzzle to Rachel.

"I'm going to miss Oscar, Rachel," my father said. "We had many good times, in and out of the office." He then kissed Rachel on the cheek.

"The office won't be the same without him, Rachel." He raised his glass,

"Here's to you, old friend."

"Thank you, Ralph," she said as news of the assassination of Treasury Secretary Mitchel Snipes came across the TV. We had all heard the first broadcast but paused to watch this one, listening for anything new. Rachel's legal mind was working, trying to figure out who might have done it. Only one person didn't come to show his respects, Senator Thomas Florin. Dad and I stayed a while talking to several of the people we knew.

Many professionals arrived to pay their respects, some from the Courts, some from State Congress. A couple of past clients came to get a free lunch. We watched and thanked them for coming. Dad asked me about New Hampshire and how I liked it. I told him,

"It's good, dad. You should come up for a visit. I think you'd enjoy the ride. I know you'd like Lakes Crossing. It's a pretty little town on the edge of a big lake."

He paused to sip on his scotch. "I think I'd take the Mercedes; it's more reliable than the Chrysler."

"Well, yeah, I would think so. The Chrysler is 40 years old, and the Mercedes has had more storage time than road time." I raised my glass and quietly offered, "and you can even bring Veronica with you."

"Oh, you, the cop, always suspecting something. I'll have you know Veronica and me share an amicable, working relationship. She is very good at what she does." He said coyly.

"It's okay, dad. I approve. It's time you had a cozy relationship again. In fact, I think mom would approve."

"Do you really think so, son? I would hate to do anything to taint her memory."

"Come on up, dad, and bring Veronica with you. I would love to have you see where I work. You might be able to give me a few tips."

"Help you with your case, you mean? How is that going?"

"Art Williams and Howard Reynolds have moved up to New Hampshire. You remember them, don't you?"

"Yes, I do," Dad recalled. "I hope they enjoy it as much as you do. Have you said hello to them yet?"

"Yes and No. Right now, the 'accidental' death of Reynolds's wife has me wondering about Art Williams' involvement. The M. E. tells me she was murdered, injected with a very potent sedative. She could have been dead before she went down the stairs. I have to talk to Art Williams about it. He was a very welcome visitor, but I think he might have been a little too welcome.

"Is he suspected of killing the wife?"

"I don't know. There's nothing that says Art did it, or Howie did it or anyone else for that matter.

Art's always been the odd duck, but I never would suspect him of doing anything like this. Since he's been home from Nam, though, he's a different guy. His parents noticed it right away. "He's not the same boy," they told me."

"And a relationship with Sandy Reynolds seems way out of line. She and Howie married shortly before moving there after Howie returned from Nam. He's not the same either after Nam. The war screwed them up a bit."

"WhenSandy started writing for Guns & Ammo, she made a lot of trips to gun shows and competitions. They were her subjects. It was at one of the shows that she met Williams, and that might have been where the suspicions of a relationship started."

"But after ten years, and she's dead already? Strange." dad added.

"Yeah, ten years. What I found odd was Sandy's death coming on the coattails of the Conklin and Snipes assassinations. Why would she die then?"

"Are you thinking there's a connection? How could there be?" dad asked.

"I don't know, dad. It's one of those feelings you get when you think you're right, but you're not sure you want to be, like an itch you can't scratch."

"Watch those itches, son. You scratch too much, and you can get yourself into trouble."

Rachel came by and asked,

"Grant, I meant to ask you about your dog. What kind is it?"

"Oh, an English Boxer. Buster Piddle is almost two years old. I rescued him when I left Rhode Island. I'll watch him grow into a police dog for Lakes Crossing. He might not meet the height requirements or finish the quarter-mile in record time, but he will not get fat and lazy. Buster will do everything I do as far as police work is concerned. I'm going to send him to school to learn to be a cop, and he's going to teach me how to use the hydrant."

Rachel laughed, and I fell in love with her right there. But she broke the spell with, "Stop in to see me the next time you're in the area. Here's my business card. Call if you need any help with a case or even personal reasons."

That was something I didn't expect.

"Thank you, Rachel. I'll do that."

Now I had two bites of the apple, I thought.

"You call me if you need any help down here."

Dad sipped his scotch while his eyes were rolling my way,

"Take the hint, son. You won't get a better offer than that."

"Dad! I can take care of my personal life. Thank you." "*Oh, what you don't know, dad,*" I said to myself. We finished our drinks and said goodbye.

"Veronica, where are you, lovely lady?" I asked. I wanted to say goodbye and extend my invitation to her whenever she could get my father to bring her up.

CHAPTER 18

Domino #3

Attorney General Albert Howe is a lover of venison. More is his love of getting his own, in or out of season. And any mountain or hill in New England will usually get him what he wants to fill his freezer. Since the assassination of Archie Conklin, security has doubled for members of the President Cabinet.

In hunter camo, six Secret Service agents guarding Howe were dressed like the attorney general.

They were spaced out less than 50 yards from him when a doe with a new fawn was spotted in a small clearing. All the agents freeze in place, waiting for Howe to take the shot and claim his prize.

After a full minute, the deer begin to move. The guards wonder why Howe hasn't fired. The deer run into the woods and disappear. Another thirty seconds go by before the guards go to Howe's location and find him slumped over in the brush, an arrow through his neck. A domino has fallen beneath his collar, with a note attached.

**"Three down, Mr. President.
How many more do you want me to take?"**

The White House is immediately notified, and the President is placed under extra security. Every move President Comstock makes will now go under the FBI's microscope.

"What in God's blue heaven is going on? Now my Attorney General is dead? How could that happen? How could three of my closest confidants all be assassinated in one year? Hell, in two months? How in blazes am I going to run this country with all my advisors getting picked off around me?"

FBI Director Vaines hands Comstock the note that came off the arrow.

"What's this, another note?" He reads, "I've got three..."and another domino? Why, the balls of this guy, taunting me. Has any information been gotten on the shooter? Is it even the same guy? Has Forensics been able to get anything?" He raves.

"Nothing yet, sir," Vaines tells the President.

"How does this guy know where my people are before they get there? Hell, even I don't know where they go when they leave here," the President said. "There's a Benedict Arnold walking around Congress. I want every bit of communication recorded in this office analyzed, scrutinized, and taken apart. From now on, no one is to be trusted. I'm going to get this little bastard if it's the last thing I do."

A woman walking a little gray dog makes her way down the grassy path off Rounds Mountain.

She throws a compound bow into the brush on her left and the quiver to her right. Her black Ford pickup is in the parking lot. The Park Ranger receives a garbled message on his radio that someone on top of the mountain needs assistance. He stops to question the lady.

"Excuse me, miss. Did you see anyone else on the trail today?"

"No, not today. We walked most of the mountain, stopped a few times, had lunch. But, no, no other hikers out today. I usually see a couple or two, but today, the mountain was all mine. It's pretty up there. I'm coming back again in the Fall when the colors are out. Well, got to go." She places the dog in the cab and drives away.

CHAPTER 19

Rocking The Cradle

Following A.G. Howe's death, rumors run through the House and the Senate of the President, possibly resigning and passing the hat onto Vice-President Holloway.

"Who's next?" asked Transportation Secretary Rockwell Timer.

"Don't start that game going around," says Secretary of Energy Bernard Ohman and Secretary of Commerce Timothy Workman. The three are seriously passing the idea around to the other members of Congress of asking the President to step down. Their conversation slowly makes its way to the Oval Office, and President Comstock decides to call Congress to Chamber to control the rumors of his resignation.

Buster and I didn't make the journey home that day. We stayed at dad's place and took him out to breakfast at the *Tasty Toast*. Everyone in the restaurant was getting ready to watch President Comstock's early morning Press Briefing. Dad leaned over and whispered,

"Someone is trying to force the President to either quit or stand in front of a bullet."

"My fellow Americans, despite the recent deaths...I'll say it, the assassinations of several members of my Cabinet, I am not entertaining

the idea of resigning, though I'm sure the Democrats would find that quite to their liking. The deaths of Senator Archie Conklin, Secretary Mitchel Snipes, and his wife, and now, I understand, my Attorney General, Albert Howe, were three men indispensable to me in keeping this country running on an even keel. I'll not have any difficulty filling their positions and keeping this ship of state sailing on as before. I am asking Congress to move earnestly and quickly in passing the bills that make lead to the most significant advantage to the American people."

As the President's speech began to sound like the same old bullshit he had been feeding the country, everyone turned back to their breakfast, the clinking of silverware on dinner plates presuming their boredom.

"Do you see a pattern, son?" Dad asked. "All the President's Men, the ones that pull strings, one by one, someone is taking them out. How many more will have to die before the shooter gets what he wants? I see someone trying to force a shift in the voting in Congress, and the Democrats will take the hit for it. Comstock won't let that change happen no matter what. He's that selfish. Someone is writing that history. It's going to be interesting to see who will be left to write about."

"Are you thinking there's a plot to eliminate the President?"

"Maybe they don't want to kill him. Maybe they just want to force him out." Dad surmises.

"Vice-President Holloway does not share Comstock's ideas anymore. He has made some changes since the election, and Comstock knows it. With Holloway leaning in the opposite direction, Comstock has got to be pissed off, big time. We will have to wait and see what Comstock is going to do. In the meantime, you're heading back to solve a crime of your own?"

"Yes. It's a murder case, and that makes it complicated.

"Still no clues, son?"

"Nothing."

"Pushed a little harder against those instincts of yours,' you might open a path to follow."

"What do you mean, dad?"

"Lean on Williams a little, or just go up and ask him. Let him know you're investigating him. He will tell you, no, he didn't do it. But that might trip him up into making a mistake."

"I see what you mean. Something doesn't make sense, yet it fits like it belongs there. I have to find a way to take them apart."

"Gently, son. Remember, Art Williams, is a different man now, unpredictable."

"You're right, dad. I'll start easy and see what moves."

CHAPTER 20

Token Dead

On Monday, Dad called me from the Duck. I could hear the swizzle stick tingling in his glass. He didn't ask me to drive down, but something told me I should have. He was slowly explaining a phone call he received an hour ago from the State Police,

"Your client is dead, Ralph. You can retire now." It was Chief January. The two knew one another from way back, and Homer had to be the messenger.

"What? Homer, what are you talking about? Roberts is dead."

"I guess you didn't see it on the television, huh? It happened this morning, around noon. It made for one hell of a Fourth of July on the Plaza."

"I don't understand, Homer. I was in court with him yesterday," dad explained.

"Yeah, someone got wind of the transfer and didn't want Roberts going back to Canada. They shot him on the Plaza in front of City Hall. They also wounded a State Trooper."

"Do you know who did it, Homer?"

"Not yet, Ralph. We don't have much to go on right now. I'm sorry, Ralph."

"Me, too, Homer, me, too. Thanks."

I was at a loss for words. Dad was looking forward to a wiz-bang trial before retiring. Now he'll get to retire a little earlier.

"It was a kick in the gut, son. A real kick in the gut."

"I don't know what to say, dad."

"But why would anyone want to shoot Roberts? His story wasn't anything to write home about.

It certainly didn't go anywhere that would lead to this. Was there something he didn't tell me? I suppose I should be a little upset. I had an outstanding defense prepared for him, maybe the best I've ever written. Now I won't get the chance. Damn."

I tried to show some compassion for dad's 'loss.'

"Save it, dad. You can present your case when you come to visit. I'd love to hear it."

"Really, Grant? Okay, I'll do that."

After we hung up, I thought about what dad told me in court, that he had heard someone was out to kill Roberts. There was no evidence, just voices heard while walking the corridors of City Hall. I called Rachel to find out what she knew of the shooting.

"Yes, John Roberts was killed on the Mall. An assassin from a perch somewhere in one of the buildings also shot a State Trooper. They think there was more than one shooter. Some said they heard more than one report, but it could have been the firecrackers," she explained.

"Why would somebody want to kill Roberts?" I asked. "He wasn't much of a target, and he didn't do anything that would pose a threat to anyone. It doesn't make any sense. You know, my father heard rumors about someone out to get him."

"Did your father say anything about those rumors? Who might have been doing the talking?"

"No, but he heard them again, at the Courthouse. He couldn't pinpoint who was passing it around. A couple of senators talked about justice slipping away and that someone would have to pay for the crimes gone unpunished. It was all kind of vague, that's about it." I told her.

"Strange, you mentioned the rumors before; I heard something similar on the way to my office;

secretaries talking about somebody getting killed, but no one mentioned who the target was."

"I guess we know, now, huh? Listen, if you get anything further on Williams, would you let me know?"

"Oh, yes. I will. What are you thinking, Grant? That he might have something to do with the death of John Roberts?" she asked.

"Art Williams made Expert-Marksman in the Army and only sharpened that skill in Nam. One of the weapons was a sniper rifle, and it would have taken an expert shooter to make the shot across the Mall, right? It would have taken two expert shooters to get both Roberts and the trooper."

"So, you're telling me there was another shooter out there we have to be looking for?" Rachel asked.

"Yes, I'm afraid so, Rachel. Only two shooters would allow enough time to get off the roof or wherever they perched. I have been trying to think of someone Art Williams knew with the same skills, but no one comes to mind."

"That all makes sense, but how do I find that second shooter? Art is the only one in the picture right now."

"The only possible accomplice would be Sandy Reynolds. She wrote for Guns & Ammo Magazine. She had her own weapon, and she traveled to the competitions where Art Williams competed. I don't know if Sandy competed with Williams or not. I'm going to bet she did. How else would she know what to write about while attending the matches? I'll get back to you, Rachel. I've got more work to do."

CHAPTER 21

The Patriot Spy

Jonathan peeked into Thom Florin's office, wondering why the Senator was so jittery. It was getting close to his lunch hour, and he remembered his call from Rachel to meet her at Crusty's. He walked over to Thom's office and told him,

"I'm going out for lunch. Would you like me to bring something back for you?"

"No, that's alright. Thanks for asking. Enjoy your lunch."

Jon left the office after turning on the recording device for phone calls. Walking down Frances Street, he ducked into Crusty's Bakery and walked down to the back booth where Rachel was seated. "Hi, Rachel."

"Can I get a grilled cheese with tomato, please, with fries and a Coke?" he told the waitress.

"I just heard the strangest phone call from somebody claiming to be Thom Florin's brother in New Hampshire."

"Thom has no siblings," Rachel says. "From New Hampshire, he said. I saw Grant Smalley at dad's funeral. He is the Chief of Police in the same town Howard Reynolds, and Art Williams live in."

"I know Grant," Jon said. "Do you think he might be of some help to you?"

"I don't know how Jon. Williams is suspected of murder up there. But, if Art Williams is talking to Thom Florin, there's got to be something going on. It sounds like a class reunion, but not the kind I want to attend. Williams, Reynolds, Grant, Florin, and I are all from Mt. Valle. I hope it's only coincidental.

"This is getting confusing, Rachel. Art Williams must be a very busy guy. Senator Florin is the President of the shooting club I belong to in South Kingston, and Williams is a member. It's a little out of the way, don't you think, for a guy living in New Hampshire to travel down here to shoot?" Jon paused and dipped his fries in the ketchup. Rachel asked him,

"Can you find out how often this 'brother' calls the Senator and is Tippy still at the bridge?"

Tippy is a retired CIA operative with nothing better to do.

"Yes, I can get hold of him for you if you want."

"No. I'll go to the bridge."

"Oh," Jon says with surprise. "You know about the bridge."

"I know many things, Jonathan, both legal and illegal, but this time I need to know more."

"Yes, of course." Jon then tells Rachel a secret. "Did I tell you I have a recording device under my desk?"

"You do know those are illegal, Jon?" She asked.

"Yes. But under extenuating circumstances...."

Rachel interrupted, "They are still illegal, Jon." She paused, then asked, "What did you find out?"

"Well, the Senator doesn't know it's there. I turned it on as I left. He tried to call that same New Hampshire number this morning. When the party didn't pick up, he slammed the phone down."

"Interesting. I would like to hear that conversation when the party does respond."

Rachel excused herself and walked back to her office. Jonathan ordered a bagel sandwich and a coffee for the Senator and headed back to his office.

"Here you are, Senator. You have to have something for lunch." Jon left the sandwich with Florin and returned to his desk. The phone rang.

"Senator Florin's office. Jonathan speaking. How can I help you today?"

The voice was low, attempting a disguise. "I need to speak to the Senator, please."

"Whom shall I say is calling?"

"It's his brother from New Hampshire."

Jonathan looks at the phone, that brother again. He buzzes Thom's office,

"Yes, Jonathan."

"Your brother from New Hampshire is on line one."

"My bro…oh, okay. I'll take it," Thom says. Florin gets up and closes his door.

"Hey, brother," the voice calls out.

"You idiot," Thom calls him. "I told you never to call me here."

"I just wanted to let you know I'm caught up on my work. Got anything else that needs attention?"

"Right now? No, but I will need to complete a job before the end of the month. Are you up to it?"

"Yeah, I'm good, but I've got a few things here to take care of first. I don't want my chores backing up."

"Hold tight after you do. I'll call when my tasks are complete, and we can plan the next project."

CHAPTER 22

The Other Roberts & Tippy, Too

Rachel wonders, *"I wonder what happened to Jack Roberts? First, he was on the road, then Canada and college. Now, he's in D.C. protesting for Senator Thomas Florin, wearing Florin's slogan T-shirt. But what does 'Let the Dominoes Fall' mean in a political rally? It doesn't make sense as a campaign slogan."*

"And that phony file, what did it prove to be worth? One John Roberts is dead, and the other is protesting. All is right with the world." Rachel ordered her aid to shred the file.

Jon called to tell her,

"The Senator got a call from his brother in New Hampshire, again. He got a little testy over it.

The conversation is on the recording device."

"I'm betting Art Williams was on the other end of that line." Rachel guesses.

"He is kind of a wild card. I've seen him at the Crosshairs Shooting Club. He takes his shooting very seriously and hates to go up against competitors that aren't *'worth a bullet,'* I've heard him say.

He and Senator Florin have been in discussion many times," Jon tells her. Rachel asked, "Do you have any idea what's going on?"

"Florin came to the club one Saturday afternoon, acting pretentious, drunk, complaining about the legal system. *Criminals are getting light sentences or getting away with murder,'* he would rant. So, he started a little side club called the Justice Temple.

"Only qualified members can join my expert shooters. It would help if you had a lot of free time."

A couple of ex-Marines were eager to get in on it.

"Art Williams joined up to sharpen his long-distance shots. A young lady signed on, also, to hone her marksmanship downrange. I don't remember her name, but she was a pretty redhead. She stayed close to Williams, and like him, she was an excellent marksman with all the weapons, pistol, target rifle; imposing."

"What did you mean by, *were,* a couple of ex-Marines. Did some backout?" Rachel asked.

"No, well, we don't know. The three were very active in the Club. They were given 'assignments,'

according to Thom Florin. Then, all of a sudden, they were gone, never attending another meeting. They didn't just get up and leave. One by one, they stopped coming to the meetings."

"And Thom Florin gave out assignments?"

"Yes. He would pick some of us to research the targets; find out their calendars, where they would be at certain times. Then he would assign the best shooter, by turn, to go out and do the job."

"Can you say, 'do the killing,' Jon? Thom Florin would assign someone to go out and kill a member of the Congress of the United States. Is that what you mean?"

"I won't swear to the accuracy of your statement, Rachel. I did not know the outcome of any of the assignments until that shooter returned. And even then, the assignment was never talked about."

Rachel hung her head in disappointment. Her friend, Jon Adams, the son of her friend Tippy Adams, had all but confessed to his involvement in the assassinations of Conklin and Snipes.

"What did you do, Jon? Did you go out on any of these 'assignments?' She asked.

"No, Rachel, I did not go out. My job at the club is more as a secretary. I keep the books, greet the members and guests as they come in. I plan the President's calendar."

Rachel's eyebrows rose at the mention of the calendar. She looked at Jon but said nothing.

"I'll save that for later," she thought.

Jon told her, "A car belonging to one of the Marines was abandoned in a parking lot by the college where he worked. But no one knows where he is. You might try talking to Homer, Rachel. He might know something."

"I'll do that. Thank you for the information you've given me. Keep watching Florin for me, and keep that tape machine running. I have a feeling it will come in handy. Thom doesn't have to know any of this, right, Jon?"

"He doesn't know a thing," Jon revealed.

"You said there was a young woman who joined this 'Justice Temple,' also?"

"Yes. I don't remember her name. I would have to go through the membership roster. The men in the club talked about how good a shot she was and would not compete against her."

"Interesting. Grant might like to know that," Rachel summarized. "Okay, keep things hush with the Senator. I don't want him to know. I'm seeing your father today to find out what he might have for me. He's still at the bridge, Jon?"

"Yes, he is. How long have you known of the bridge, Rachel."

"You understand if there are some things I don't tell people," she said.

"Yes, I do. For concern for my father, I have said nothing about what he does, where he goes, or where he stays. I am surprised he tells me some of the things I think he shouldn't tell me, but I guess it's his trust in me that allows him to do that."

"Just try to avoid suspicion, Jon. I know Thom will pick up on that," Rachel said.

"I'll do my best," he said.

"You know, now, that your father is going to be alright. Take some comfort in that, but leave the law, leave us to do our work. We will get Art and Thom Florin and put an end to whatever they've been doing. You just go back to work and act as though nothing has happened. That will be a big help to us. Keep that recorder going."

"Ok?" Rachel said.

Jon looked into her eyes and saw her determination and resolve. "Alright. I'll do it. I want to see them hang."

"The doctor knows to inform me of Tippy's condition. I will then call you. Don't worry." Rachel kissed Jon on the cheek and sent him back to work.

"Now I've got to tell Grant our two cases are connected. But I want to know how and why."

CHAPTER 24

Contemplating Suspects

Back in her office, Rachel started filling in the holes in the case of Florin and Williams. She knew Art was guilty of the attempted murder of C.I.A. Agent Tippy Adams. The F.B.I. file on Roberts that fell on her desk proved to be a fake. Tippy gave Florin accurate information, but Florin took it and made it a hodgepodge of phony facts. The Senator wanted to make sure the right Roberts got his due.

"One Roberts got it, right or wrong. What did that mean, she questioned? She lay all the suspicions out on paper."

"The Roberts from Oregon led a hard life scratching the earth with his father. The other Roberts, who attended Mt. Valle with us, came from Georgia. His father left money for John, enough that he didn't want for anything. By coincidence, they both ended up in Canada but through totally different circumstances. But why kill one Roberts and not the other? Why kill either of them?"

After talking to Homer, Rachel had what she needed to fill in John Roberts's file. A light bulb went on when she read the name of the old gent Roberts killed, Howard Florin, Lt. Colonel Howard Florin; recipient of the Purple Heart and the Bronze Star with Cluster. Colonel Florin was Thomas Florin's father, who had retired to Watertown, New York after his wife died. And Lt. Colonel Howard Florin succumbed as a result of his injury."

"Now, I have the reason for Roberts' assassination and by whom!" Rachel concluded. But she knew Thomas Florin didn't pull the trigger. She had to have proof, though, that he was involved in the shooting. She thought of Ralph Smalley, the lawyer assigned to defend John Roberts, and gave him a call.

"Ralph Smalley, Attorney at Law. This is Veronica; how can I help you?"

"Veronica, it's Rachel Biggar. Is Ralph in? I need to speak to him."

"Yes, he is, Rachel. Just a moment; I'll connect you."

"Hello, Rachel. What can I do for you today?"

"Ralph, with the death of your client, you are free to divulge anything he might have told you in confidence. I need to know, Ralph, what happened on his escape route."

Ralph told Rachel all that John Roberts revealed. Their conversation lasted 45 minutes, long enough for her to approach Thomas Florin with certain questions. But she didn't go. She instead called Grant to tell him what she found and warn him to be cautious around Art Williams.

CHAPTER 25

A Senate Call

Secretary of State Elizabeth Beane stood at the podium to address Congress. She first reads the front-page headline in the Washington Post,

"Attorney General Albert Howe found murdered hunting in New York."

"Mr. President, my fellow members of Congress, I just read to you the latest headline in today's Washington Post. It's no secret an assassin has targeted our President's closest defenders, those of you that have backed his opposing stance against Democratic proposals. It appears more than coincidental that your positions on Justice, Treasury, and First Nation have not changed due to the shootings. Whoever is eliminating these members of your cabinet may eventually choose to get more personal until those policies change positively. I will say to those members of this body; your votes are harming our country, resulting in riots in every major city, causing

irrefutable damage that may be difficult to turn around and repair. Mr. President, there could be a fair and politically decent solution, your resignation."

The Chamber erupts as the Secretary steps down. Secretary to Veterans Affairs, Admiral Samuel Cortez, and Secretary of Homeland Security, Robert White Feather, stand at the podium to address the Chamber. Slowly, the din diminishes, and Congress recognizes their fellow members. Sec. White Feather speaks,

"My esteemed colleagues of this great body of lawmakers. We have the power to make a change in this country, to better the lives of the people we serve, and yet, we allow one individual to make the change that does not serve the people but serves him alone. The lies, the cheating, the theft of privileges, signing declarations that enrich his pockets because he believes he has the right to do so as President."

"The land on which my people live, originally belonging to them, was stolen by this government, murdering, raping and pillaging, village by village, Nation by Nation. Today, the people starve for lack of food and the essentials for a decent living and the pride and honor of a homeland stolen from them. They seek stability, opportunity, and aid in essential services, such as medicine and education.

Why do we not assist them? Look to the enemies we defeated in wars around the world. In Germany, Japan, Italy, Vietnam' we helped rebuild them, and they thrive today. But we do nothing to help rebuild our First Nation. If they have oil? We federalize it. Precious minerals? We rape the land and leave them nothing. Is it the aim of this government to wipe out these peoples from the face of the earth?"

"Think of what we are doing. Up to now, we haven't been doing anything worthwhile. The First Nation, our

beginnings; we owe them a chance to live their way of life and not be burdened by lawless and greedy people. Perhaps more than one man has chosen to fight corruption so blatantly enlivened by certain individuals of this body, who have now been eliminated. I know, and you know others may be subjected to the same fate. I will say the process is wrong and must be stopped. That person keeps us from making the changes our country needs by assassinating those members that could do our nation good."

"The difficulties we face, serving our constituents, serving our country, honoring our oath to serve, because of the few who serve our President wrongly, we must change. Let us pray an assassin's bullet is not the way to stop this President and those whose greed has led them to follow him. You know those sitting beside you who have failed to speak up and confront the President. It is time to do so, ladies and gentlemen before we lose more members. It is time."

The Chamber is silent as Admiral Cortez takes the podium. Sparkling white in uniform, medals reflecting the lights in the Chamber, he begins,

"I cannot address you as eloquently as my friend, Secretary White Feather. I shall be brief. To the parties involved in the assassinations of the members of the President's Cabinet, I ask you to stop. I believe I understand the motives behind your actions, but I know you can reach your goal without further bloodshed. I ask you to contact me, or Secretary White Feather, directly. Our communications will be in the strictest confidence. Should you choose an emissary as your contact, we will accept that."

The Chamber made no sound as Cortez and White Feather left the building. Cortez tells White Feather and the media in the hallway,

"I hope, whoever it is, heard us. I don't know if it was enough; only that individual will know.

Perhaps he will want more; we don't know that, either." He and White Feather walk away from the mics.

"You did good, Sam. I just hope the Chamber heard you. The killing has to stop, and we must do what we can to stop it," White Feather tells him.

"Thanks, Bob," Sam says. "I would like you to be here when this guy shows up."

CHAPTER 26

Help In New Hampshire

"*If Thom Florin knew the man in custody killed his father, he would want revenge,*" Rachel thought, calling Grant.

"Lakes Crossing Police, Corporal Holiday speaking. What can I do for you?"

"Corporal, this is Rhode Island States Attorney General Rachel Biggar. Is your Chief available?"

"The Chief went out to visit Art Williams. He should be back shortly. Can I leave him a message?"

"Yes. Have him call me as soon as he gets in, would you? Thank you."

Chief Smalley:

"Rachel? Sorry I missed your call. What's up?" I asked her.

"Grant, I have a dirty Senator, Thom Florin, and I believe you have a dirty neighbor, Art Williams.

"Talk between the two has resulted in the death of John Roberts. Homer January told me the old veteran, Roberts assaulted during his escape, was Thom Florin's father. The man died two days later, one day before Roberts' assassination. I know Thom put two and two together, Grant, and used Art as his shooter. Who shot the State Trooper? I don't know, but it could have been one of Art's friends from the Crosshairs Sportsman's Club."

"Are you ready to move on Florin?" I asked.

"No. I need a tighter knot between the two. I can connect Williams to the attempted murder of a CIA agent, but I need more information about the Senator and his shooter," Rachel adds.

"I've been watching Williams," I told her. "Trying to match bits and pieces of his comings and goings with different events. Several days on Sandy Reynolds'calendar match the dates Williams was not in town. Reynolds told me his wife met Williams at competitions for which she was writing articles. The calendar says they were in Burlington, Vermont, for one match. But they did not attend that match, and Snipes was assassinated that same weekend."

"The calendar also marks a competition in Rounds, New York. They don't hold shooting matches in Rounds. I believe it was Sandy Reynolds that made the hit on Howe. Her husband told me after they moved to New Hampshire, she became heavily involved in outdoor sports and became very proficient with the bow. He said she was outstanding with it. Howe was killed with an arrow through the neck, right?" I asked.

"Yes, he was," Rachel concurred.

"Art Williams was in Lakes Crossing the same day Sandy took her fall, but I still haven't been able to tie him to the fall. I've got to talk to Howard Reynolds again."

CHAPTER 27

Senator Florin's Office

"Come on, pick up the phone." Florin cursed the non-person on the other end of the line.

"That bastard said he was going to be home today. Shit!" then he slammed the phone down.

Jonathan heard the noise and got up to see what had happened.

"Everything alright, Senator?"

"Yes, Jonathan. Everything is fine. I just couldn't get through to my party on the other end. I'll try again later."

"I can do that for you if you like, sir."Jonathan offers.

"No!" snaps Florin. "That's alright, Jon. I can get it later, thanks."

Sliding back and forth in his chair, Florin was nervous, wondering where Art Williams was. The schedule of missions must be on time. Jonathan checked the electronic phone register in the outer office and recorded the last call. He calls Rachel to meet her at Crusty's.

"Not today, Jon. I've got a plateful to sort through. What have you got?"

"The Senator just tried to call Art Williams. Williams wasn't home." Jon told her.

"Shit, where is he off to now?" she wonders.

Senator Florin wondered the same thing. "There's only one mission remaining, and only one Marine left to do the work. That jarhead better get it right."

Florin turned on the television to watch Comstock's address before Congress. A reporter's microphone catches the conversation between White Feather and Cortez.

Thom Florin summarizes, "Well, somebody in Washington has been paying attention to what I've been doing. Calling Art off the scent is not going to be easy. He's got to call me back, and soon." He called Jon into his office.

"Jon, how is my calendar for the next three weeks?"

Jon flips through the calendar. "Let me see…two meetings with the Finance, one with Highway about the Pike repairs, and a couple of school Fall outings. Other than that, you're good for a day or three off." Jon tells him.

"Alright. Set up a meeting with Homeland Security, something on the Q.T. Tell the people I'm out of the office for a couple of days."

"Anytime in particular?" Jon asks.

"I just need a couple of days. Make the arrangements and get back to me."

CHAPTER 28

Domino #4

In his hometown of Pavillion, NY, Secretary of the Interior Alexander Bonds celebrates Halloween with his neighbors, going house to house, scaring up treats. He walks between the houses hoping to surprise some unsuspecting child, but as he rounds the corner of one home, he falls into the shrubbery. Children think it's a Halloween prank and rush to see the 'body.' One little girl touches the Secretary, and he falls to the ground. She screams when she spots blood coming from his neck. Secret Service rushes in to find two bullet holes in the back of the neck. The spine is severed, and the bullets exit through the throat. The Secretary is dead, and the alert goes out to the other agents. In the dark, amongst all the revelers in costume, the chief agent tells his men,

"Cordon off the neighborhood, the entire village, all roads in and out. Get a chopper up from Batavia, and see if Dansville has one. Tell them to watch for any vehicle leaving the town at a high rate of speed." An ambulance pulls up, and the coroner pronounced Bonds dead. They turn the body over to find a domino on the ground under him. A note attached to the domino reads,

"#4 Mr. President. Watch your mailbox."

The note and domino are placed in a plastic bag and turned in as evidence. The President, dumbfounded, can not believe that someone has murdered four of his most trusted Cabinet members and has gotten away with it.

"How did anyone know he was going home for Halloween? Isn't Pavillion a small farming town in the middle of nowhere, and someone was able to get to him? Where the hell was the Secret Service, the FBI, the local police? Doesn't any law enforcement agency give a damn about protecting our public servants?" Comstock turns to Alex Vaines,

"I want every member of my Cabinet shadowed, cloaked; I don't care how you do it, 24 hours a day. I want them covered if they go anywhere, even the shit house. Do you understand?"

"Yes, Mr. President."

A blue Volvo leaves Pavillion on its way north to I-90 East. A motel on the east side of Albany gives him cover for the night. He'll be in Providence later the following morning.

Along The Lake

Buster and I took a run along the lake, trying to get 5 miles in before breakfast. My mind can't let go of the puzzle the Reynolds case has become. What I had was a hodge-podge of the most apparent facts;

1) Art and Sandy were having an affair, maybe.
2) They went to competitions together, pretty sure.
3) Sandy's calendar says she and Art were in Vermont, competing when Snipes was murdered. Not true.
4) There were two shooters in Providence. I feel certain one was Art Williams. Was Sandy the other?
5) Florin's been talking to Williams a lot lately; Why?
6) Sandy's got something on somebody. That may be what got her killed, but who and what?

Sandy's death had me chasing my tail. Wondering if Howard Reynolds would see me without his lawyer, I took a chance and drove over.

"Hello, Howard." He was outside watering his lawn.

"Oh, hello, Grant," he didn't sound glad to see me.

"Is it alright if we talk a bit, Howie, without your lawyer?"

"That will depend on the questions," he said bluntly.

"Well, you know I don't believe you killed your wife. Don't you?"

"Yes. So? Have you found the guy that did?"

"I have my suspicions, Howie, but I need to get into Sandy's things."

"Why? I didn't want to disturb any of it. You can understand that, I think. And now you want to turn it all upside down. No! Go away."

"Howard. You want to find the killer as much as I do. Help me out, here. Let me see the things she left behind. I have a feeling Sandy left clues that will tell me who the killer is."

He continued watering his lawn. He glanced over at me sternly, wondering if he should allow me to interrupt Sandy's memory, then gave in.

"Are you gonna ask me to identify the things she left behind?"

"Probably, yes," I told him.

He led me into the house and the bedroom. There was a photo on top of a dresser I found interesting. It was of four men standing with Sandy at a shooting event. The names of all were printed on the bottom of the photo.

"Do you know this photo, Howard? Where was it taken?" I asked.

"That was in Rhode Island, at a competition the Crosshairs Sportsman Club was having. I never met the three men on the left, but Senator Thom Florin is standing next to Sandy on the right. You remember him. He graduated from Mt. Valle with us. I understand he's running for President in the next election." Howard explained.

Running for President, a perfect reason to discredit the current President.

"Do you mind if I borrow this?" I asked. *Sandy is standing with Senator Florin; interesting*, I thought.

"No, you can have it. I never liked the picture anyway."

He allowed me to browse through the closet. I found a box of items on the floor, loose things, like spare change you might take out of your pocket.

I found the rifle *Guns & Ammo Magazine* had given her; it was beautiful. Sandy took good care of it.

"Is this all of it, Howard? After how many years of writing?" I looked at Howard and asked, "Did you throw anything out, Howard?"

"No. And as far as her writings are concerned, there are a couple of books she wrote downstairs on the shelf and several of her *Guns & Ammo* magazines where her articles were featured. These are the personal things I couldn't throw out." He shied back and sat on the bed with a mournful look.

Howard explained the various things I held up to him. I found nothing I would call a clue, so we went to the living room. Howard showed me the magazines he couldn't discard. I rifled through a couple of them, seeing pictures of Sandy as the featured writer. One magazine was different. When I opened it, a letter fell out. It was sealed and addressed to me. Showing it to Howard, he said,

"I wonder why she would address a letter to you?' he asked.

I slit the seal and began to read. The letter sounded like a last *Will* & *Testament*, combined with a confession of sins, implicating certain people in the assassinations of members of Congress. I was not surprised to find Art Williams' and Senator Thomas Florin's names associated with those same deaths. I looked at Howard as I finished reading the letter and excused myself without revealing what I found.

"Thank you, Howard. You don't know how much you and Sandy have helped this investigation."

I rifled through other magazines, and a second letter fell out addressed, *'I'm sorry, Howie.'* I immediately knew it was a personal confession to Howard, her husband.

As I left, Howie exclaimed,

"Somebody killed my wife, Grant!"

I turned and told him, "I promise you, Howie, I will bring the killer to justice." I knew he was angry, but it wasn't at me or the police. He was mad at the killer. He was angry thinking of the person who did it, which used to be a friend. One that graduated high school with him ten years ago. He was mad at himself for not seeing what others saw when Art and Sandy spent time together at the competitions. And it was all there, in the letter, in the confession.

It didn't matter now because I knew who killed Sandy Reynolds and why. The case is solved; it's over, as far as I was concerned. I thought of driving up to Black Cove, but I wasn't going alone. Recalling Art's military training and experience with a weapon, I had to have backup to bring him in. I called Norm and told him what I had for evidence.

CHAPTER 30

The Last Goodbye

"How are you today, Howie?" Art asked, seated at the counter. He was having breakfast with Mutts and watched Howard walk in with disbelief tattooed on his face.

"Like I got handed the shitty end of the stick, Art. I can write away times like this when it's all in my imagination," glaring at Art, "but it's real, Art, authentic, and hard to deal with this time. But you wouldn't know about those kinds of things, would you, Art?"

"What are you talking about, buddy?" Art asked.

"I've smoked too many cigars and drunk too many bottles of whiskey trying to find the answers, and I ain't never gonna see sober again." Howie was standing a bit unstable. "Then I got a letter. Sandy left it for me, and all the answers were right there, right in the letter. Yep, Sandy wrote them all down and left them for me. In a letter, tucked in one of her magazines."

"What are you talking about, Howie? Sandy wrote you a letter? About what?" Art was shocked that he was being openly exposed. His defenses were peaked. "Chief Smalley came to see me the other day, Howie. Did you know he was coming over?"

"No, I didn't know he was going to your place. So what?" Reynolds answered incredulously, "Why would I care if he was going over to see you? Unless he was going to arrest your ass!"

"Arrest my ass? For what? You've been talking to him, Howie. What did you tell him?"

"I couldn't tell him much. He was telling me!"

"You fellas can take it outside if you don't mind." The store proprietor told them.

"What did he tell you, Howie?"

"Like maybe you and Sandy had something going when she went away to those matches."

Howard's drunkenness was dragging his tongue across his lips.

Art got up and grabbed Howard's arm, dragging him outside.

"Are you gonna believe him or me? Accusing me of having an affair with Sandy? That's a flat-out lie, Howie."

"He didn't say anything specific. Only intimating that it was possible. That it did seem a little more than coincidental, that you both happened to be in the same city at the same time."

"That son-of-a-bitch. Not true, Howie. Sandy and me were not having an affair." He turned around and asked Howard, "How long have we known each other, Howie?"

Howard went up to Art, face to face, and said, "Not long enough. Sandy spelled it all out in her letter, in two letters. I'll let you figure out who has the second one."

"Alright," Art paused, "Sandy wanted me not to tell you, but she liked guns as much as I do. She even learned to shoot better than me sometimes. I was surprised when Guns & Ammo gave her that beautiful rifle. Yes, we were in the same cities simultaneously; Sandy wrote and competed in my matches. She was good, Howie. She was outstanding. But I swear to you we were not having an affair."

"So, her work for *Guns & Ammo,* did that involve firsthand knowledge, hands-on experience?"

Howard guessed, "Maybe a little coaching, too, huh, Art?"

"No, there was no coaching," Art hollered.

"Did Norma know about the competitions together? Was she suspicious of you and Sandy? The divorce wasn't just about the PTSD or the drinking, was it, Art?"

"No, it wasn't. Norma accused me, too, of cheating on her with Sandy. She even asked Sandy about it. That's when she filed for divorce. I don't know what Sandy told her. I tried to change her mind. She wouldn't listen, not to me, not to Sandy."

"Where did Sandy get her first gun?" Reynolds asked.

"She used one of mine, at first." Art told him, "Then *Guns & Ammo* gave her one."

"No matter where you competed, you knew she was my wife. You knew you had no right to take her from me."

Howard could see Art trying to hide his shame but didn't think he knew how. It didn't work. It only made things worse. There was no excuse for Art to hide behind. He and Sandy were too close on those overnight trips. Too close, and often, friends at the house, lovers on tour.

Howard left Art at the General Store and came to keep an appointment with me, not telling Art about coming to the station. The accusations made Art wonder how close Grant was getting. Art got in his car and drove by the Police station to see Howard had stopped in.

"It looks like I've got another loose end to close," he told himself.

CHAPTER 31

The Last Domino

Billie turned on the television and caught the middle of a newscast,

'Breaking News - Secretary of the Interior, Alexander Bonds, was assassinated this evening while celebrating Halloween walking the streets of his hometown in Pavillion, NY. Howe is the fourth member of President Daniel Comstock's Cabinet to be assassinated. Police have no suspects at this time.'

"Geezuz, boss," Billie says, "Now it's four members of the Cabinet. He's not going to be able to do his job without his advisors."

"He hasn't been doing it anyway," I said casually. "Whoever is doing this must have one hell of a grudge against the government. I don't know how they're getting away with it."

Turning my investigation toward Art William's and his hide-a-way off Black Island Cove, I felt Howard Reynolds was now able to see that there might be something about his wonderful wife that he didn't know. It did involve his buddy, Art Williams.

"Williams' worth seems to be a little higher than Howard Reynolds knew," I said.

"Did you see his cash flow? Good, God!" Norman exclaimed. "I wish the credit side of my ledger was this high. And look how mobile he is. He does a bit of traveling; twice to NY, once in Vermont, a couple of times in Virginia, and he gets to Providence a couple of times a month."

"And his base camp is Lakes Crossing," I said. "I've got Williams on the Sandy Reynolds murder,"

I told Norm, "But I'm calling Rachel to fill her in on what I have on him. Rachel thinks there's a connection between him and Thom Florin."

I paid a visit to Art Williams, instructing Billie that I wouldn't be long.

"If I'm not back in an hour, call Norm. He'll know what to do."

The red Ford Taurus SHO was sitting in the drive on Black Island Cove. I pulled in behind it and gazed around the place. It looked small and cozy, big enough for one man. The sun was going down, and the house began casting a long shadow. I had the evening's twilight in my face, but I could see a man about 6ft tall standing in the window. He was wearing a leather shooting jacket, smoking a cigarette.

Turning to the left, he disappeared. I guessed he was headed for the entrance door. As I went around the corner, he was standing in the doorway, waiting for me.

"Can I help you?" he asked.

"Good morning," I offered. "My name is Capt. Grant Smalley, police chief of Lakes Crossing."

"I know who you are. You were in my graduating class at Mt. Valle in Providence."

"Yes. Yes, I was. Thanks for the refresher course."

"What can I do for you, Captain?" Williams asked.

"I think you know of the death of Sandy Reynolds. She was the wife of Howard Reynolds, another graduate of Mt. Valle. Do you know anything about Sandy that might tell me how she fell down

"The conversation didn't last long," He added. " I think I ruined his breakfast, but I don't feel bad about that, not after he ruined my life."

"So, what do we need to discuss this afternoon, Howie? You gave me what I needed to arrest him and put him away for a long time. I'll have him behind bars very soon. I think you can go home now and feel justified." I sent him home, looking like he felt better about it all. But I figured that would come after he slept off the alcohol.

Three days later, I received a call from a neighbor who had been out walking his dog. He said he saw the door to Howard's house left open and that it had been that way for the last three days. He went up to inform Howard but couldn't get in because of the odor. I drove over to investigate and found the door open. I also smelled something very foul. My training told me immediately it was the smell of death. I went in with a handkerchief on my nose and walked around to the bedroom. Howard Reynolds was in bed, asleep, his head on the pillow. At least I thought he was sleeping. I could see two small bullet holes in his skull. I walked outside for fresh air, vomiting from the smell and the sight of Howard's death. I radioed Billie to call Norm and have him send a team over to go through the scene. An ambulance arrived just as Norm pulled in. His team of agents followed and entered the house with masks. They went to work gathering evidence while Norm and I went back to the station to discuss the shooting.

Norm told me, "The coroner says the weapon was most likely a .22. Since no one heard a shot, the shooter must have used a silencer."

"A .22, that rings a bell. That's what Rachel told me a murderer in Providence was using killing three Marines. If this is the work of Art Williams, he has got to be stopped, and now."

A Forensic agent came in telling us he found boot prints outside the rear door and the identical boot prints under the bed, directly under the victim's head position. They also found gun powder residue on the victim's head, sheet, and pillow around the head."

"The killer stood directly over him, and he never heard a thing," Norm concluded.

"That's a very cold thing to do to a friend. Williams is something else. We'll have to be well prepared to take him in. He shoots for the sport, and I don't want to give him a chance to put our heads on the wall."

"You have a dead woman's confession of her complicity in killing a Senator and his wife in Vermont, an Attorney General in New York, an assassination in Providence, and the name of her accomplices. You have the reason the killer finished her off, and now her husband. This guy is cleaning up loose ends. The evidence in Sandy's letter is certainly not circumstantial, but I think you need to call Rhode Island and talk to your friend."

Norm was reading the case file through his years of experience, and he and I came up with the same conclusions.

I called Rachel, "Hi, Rachel. Where are you in the case of the good Senator? I can bag Art Williams based on an accomplice's written confession."

"Whose confession would that be?" She asked.

"Sandy Reynolds. She was the second shooter in Roberts's assassination, and it was all sanctioned by the one and only Senator Thomas Florin."

Rachel added, "and I have our good Senator, a fellow graduate of Mt. Valle and the class clown, implicated in the Roberts' killing. When Thom Florin found out it was John Roberts, who killed his father, he had to get even. So, he used Art Williams, an Army sniper, to assassinate him".

"Captain January is piecing together the three Marine deaths with the activities of Williams and Florin, and he now has the link between that killing and the three Marines. So, what do you have I can use?"

"Sandy Reynolds met Thom Florin at the Crosshairs Sportsmen's Club. He introduced her to the Justice Temple and the targets he had on his docket, namely those members of Comstock's Cabinet, now dead. She confesses in her letter that she was the second shooter in the Roberts assassination."

"She also writes,

"That Thom Florin is a smart one. Setting up those three Jarheads to do his killing, then cleaning house by eliminating them.

Art Williams is damn good with a rifle, a pistol, and even his hands. He said he learned all those killing methods in the service. Williams killed Roberts at City Hall and Snipes on the boat. In private conversation, Art confessed to me that he killed the three Marines to eliminate any backwash problems. I told him I understood, and Senator Thomas Florin sanctioned it.

If Florin or Art finds out about this letter, I'll be in for a cleaning, too. I'm glad my husband doesn't know about my extracurricular activities. If he knew, he, too, would be up for cleaning as well.

I write this letter to confess to my involvement in the killings of the members of Congress, though I never pulled the trigger on any of them. Senator Thomas Florin is the mastermind, and Arthur Williams is the primary shooter. The three Marines did their job and became expendable."

A pause followed, then Rachel spoke, "Well, she knew something was coming. Now we have to close up shop and nail these two bastards before they kill anyone else."

"I've got an agent watching Williams," I told her. "There's no telling what he will do if he gets on the road."

"The FBI is about to get the evidence I have. Thom Florin is out of town right now but will be arrested when he returns. Keep in touch."

We closed the conversation with, "Good Luck."

CHAPTER 33

A D.C. Warning

Jon Adams cleared the Senator's calendar for the weekend trip.

"What are you going to do with your time away from the office?" Jon asked.

"I have an appointment in D.C. I have to keep. I'll be in trouble if I miss this one. Sorry to run out early, Jon, but I know the office is in good hands." With that, Thom left to pack for his trip.

When Jon locked up the office, he made sure the recorder was on for any messages that came in. He heard the phone ring and ran in to get it.

"Hello, Senator Florin's office. How can I help you?"

"This is the Senator's brother, from New Hampshire. Is my brother in?"

"Oh, I'm sorry. The Senator has left for the weekend and won't be back till Monday. Would you like to leave a message?"

"Just tell him I'll be in to see him."

"Is that all?"

The caller hung up. Jon remembered the Senator has no brothers and that Rachel told him the 'brother' was most likely Art Williams. He also remembered Art from the first time he visited the office. Jon let all the evidence stay on the recorder as he closed the door for the weekend.

In the late afternoon, Thom arrives at the Hayes Adams Hotel on H Street NW, in Washington, D.C., carrying two pieces of luggage. His room is on the top floor, facing the White House. Applying make-up, a mustache, and darkened eyebrows, he walks down to the dining room to a reserved table. Ordering a drink, he waits to meet with a vital member of Congress.

"No one will recognize me in this get-up," he concludes. He watches Admiral Samuel Cortez arrive, sans uniform, as requested, waves Cortez to his table. They discuss the recent assassinations of members of the President's Cabinet.

Cortez asks, "Do you want to tell me who you are? Your name, and why you are taking such drastic measures to make a change in the government?"

Thom asks, "Would you like a drink, Admiral?"

"No, thank you. Now tell me what you're doing," Cortez asks.

"No one in this country is happy with the current state of the economy, with Comstock, even. Everyone knows, the more illegal the things are the President gets away with, the richer he becomes, at the behest of the Republican Party and the rest of America. The people get poorer as a result. The price of food: milk, meat, produce, no one can afford to eat. Gasoline is going through the roof. And medicine: why does a small bottle of aspirin have to cost ten bucks? And the meds we need by prescription, it's cheaper to die if your family can afford the funeral.

The President smiles and lies through his teeth and blocks every fucking program the Democrats try to get through Congress. And the Senate won't do a damn thing about it. They won't touch him. What are they afraid of? He's just an ego-centric maniac who likes to see his picture in newspapers and television. And you ask me why am I doing these things? Let me ask you, "Why is nothing being done to counter this Republican stalemate of our Democracy? Why aren't the Democrats getting off their fat asses to confront Comstock's army? My job won't end until the last domino falls. You had better figure out who's side you're on, Admiral."

Thom gets up and downs his drink, then warns Cortez, *"Don't be a domino."*

Cortez grabs his arm, "Please, sit. Don't go yet. Let me tell you something few people in Congress know. Vice President Holloway is going to put the President out. I don't know how he's going to do it, and I don't know when, but you can't go on shooting and killing members of Congress."

"I'll tell you what," the man tells the Admiral. *"Since you entrusted me with your secret, I'll give you this. If I can stop the shooter, I will, but you've got to give me something."*

"Are you telling me you're not pulling the trigger on these men? If not you, then who?"

"That's my business. I control the who, the where, the why. What goes on in these people's heads I can't always control. But I will try to stop him."

Cortez watches the man leave and walk out the front door. He gets up to see which way the man went, and he was gone.

Very early the next morning, Thom went up to the roof carrying a McMillan Sub-Sonic sniper rifle. Finding a perch out of public view, he faces the White House. He sees the resident floor where the President lives through a high-power scope. He then screws a suppressor on the end of the barrel, aims, and fires three rounds through a window, timing his shots to the music downstairs in the ballroom. The bullets lodge in the wall in the president's hallway.

In the morning, Thom calls for his Audi and carries his bags downstairs, personally. He does not want to risk a porter finding the weapon. The valet places the bags in the trunk and hands him the keys, telling him, "Have a safe trip, Senator."

Late that afternoon, Thom Florin arrives at his office. Surprised, he finds Art William's waiting in the hallway.

"Art, what are you doing here on a Sunday? The office is closed."

"I called, and Jon told me you were out of town. I had nothing to do back home, so I thought I'd come down and surprise you. I also need to be paid. I need the money."

"Tomorrow would have been better to settle this. But you're lucky I have the money here."

Thom reached into the desk and opened the lower left drawer. He pulled out an envelope stuffed with money.

"Cash, you said, right? $10,000? You can sit and count it if you like, or if you trust me, take it with you and have fun."

Art takes the envelope and places it in the inside pocket of his jacket. Retrieving a .22 pistol from his back pocket, he puts two rounds into Thom's head and two more into his heart. Thom falls back in his office chair and dies, staring up at the man he hired to do his bidding.

Art salutes his victim and says, "Thanks for the business," then closes the door on the way out. There is no one in the building to see Art leave this Sunday afternoon. No one will hear the yellow Volkswagen pull out of the parking lot or see the faint white smoke of its exhaust, but there is a recording of his visit.

CHAPTER 34

Monday Opening

On Monday, Jon Adams unlocks the office a little earlier than his usual 0700 AM. He wants to have it up and running on time for the Senator when he returns from his weekend jaunt. He notices a light on in the Senator's office.

"Oh, Thom must have gotten back early," he thinks. *"I'll go in to say good morning."*

Jon opens the door expecting to find Senator Thomas Florin refreshed and ready to start another week, possibly with a satisfying smile on his face. He is shocked at what he sees; Thom Florin, RI State Senator, aspiring candidate for the President of the United States, slumped back in his chair, dead.

"Oh, Thom," he says. *"I guess Art got to you, too."* He calls security; they call the Capitol Police and an ambulance. His next call is to Rachel to tell her what he had found.

"It was terrible, Rachel, to see Thom dead like that. I know he was under suspicion for the killings of those Congressmen, but what could have made Art do this?"

"Take a deep breath, Jon. Are you out of Thom's office?"

"Yes. The coroner is in there along with Capitol Police. EMTs are taking the body out now."

Rachel asks, "Was the recording machine on?" Rachel asked.

"Yes. The whole thing should be on tape. I haven't checked it yet. It's a little busy around here."

"Alright, Jon. I didn't think Art would go this far. Get the tape when the office is empty and bring it to me. I have to find Art Williams. I'll call Homer January and tell him we have a tape. Don't do anything else, Jon. Let the forensics people do their work. I have to call Grant and let him know what happened. He can pick up Art Williams whenever he's ready."

"Thank you, Jon."

Lakes Crossing PD

"Good morning, Rachel. How is my favorite AG?" I asked.

"I'm glad I'm your favorite, Grant because I've got some news for you. Thom Florin is dead. Art Williams must have been here over the weekend. He left his calling card, killing Thom with a .22. It's all on tape, and I'm putting out a warrant for Williams' arrest. Pick him up, Grant, but be very careful. I don't want anything happening to you."

That last sentence caught me by surprise. I shook it off to get myself back on track.

"Don't worry, Rachel. I'll be prepared for him. State Police are standing by if he won't come peacefully. Howard Reynolds' body was found in his bed yesterday morning, shot in the head with a.22."

"A .22," Rachel asks. "Art's weapon of choice, it seems, for personal jobs, and that closes the case on the three dead Marines. They were also killed with a .22. If we could only find out the why for all these senseless killings.

"He's tying up loose ends, Rachel. He and Florin couldn't leave anyone behind to expose what they were doing. It's just that it backfired on Thom. I have it all in the letter Sandy Reynolds left me. It spells out a great deal of what Thom was up to and that Art was the primary shooter.

"Oh, that sounds too good to be true. Please be careful when you approach Williams, and let me know when it's over."

"I'll do that, Rachel. I promise."

As soon as I hung up, I told Billie to grab his weapon and the shotgun. "Elizabeth, call the State Police and tell Norm we're on our way to arrest Art Williams."

"His men should be ready to go, boss."

"We shouldn't be too long, Elizabeth," I had to remind myself I had a secretary.

"I'm all set, boss." Billie and I drove to Art's house and waited for that little yellow Volkswagen to come up the driveway.

The red SHO was parked as if primed for a get-away. I pulled alongside it. Billie and I got out and waited. It was just after noon, and Art's dog was up on the back of the sofa. That had to be a sign he was almost home, or at least, on his way.

Back at the station, Elizabeth saw a little yellow Volkswagen pull into the handicapped space.

She went out and told the driver to move to an unmarked area; otherwise, he could get a ticket. Art didn't pay attention to her. Blinded by his plan to kill Grant Smalley, overwhelmed by his killing of Howie Reynolds and Thomas Florin, blinded by the killing of the three Marines, he jumped out of his car, grabbed Elizabeth's arm, and forced her back into the station.

"Hey," she said. "What do you think you're doing?"

"We are going to sit here and wait for your Chief," Art told her. "And when he gets here, I'm going to kill him. Where did he go?"

"If you're Art Williams," she said.

"I am," he interrupted.

"He went to your place to arrest you," she told him.

"How nice," he said, almost madly. "Then perhaps we should go back to my place and surprise him. You'll like Mutts, and I know he'll like you. Let's go." He pushed her out the door to his car. She could see the .22 in his waistband and did not attempt to escape. Art wore an evil stare as they drove to Black Island Cove.

I radioed the station after waiting an hour for Art to show up. I worried when Elizabeth did not answer my call.

"Maybe she's in the Ladie's room," I thought. I was about to call again when a yellow Volkswagen Bug pulled up the drive. Art saw me immediately but did not see Billie. I told Billie to stay out of sight until Art showed up.

Art and Elizabeth exited the Bug with some caution. He then grabbed her hair and forced her in front of him.

"I understand this little girl works for you. Is that right?"

"Yes, Art, she does. Why did you get her involved in this? She's only eighteen years old. Let her go. Can't you see she's scared?" I pleaded.

"I need a bargaining chip, Grant. You're going to let me go to my car so that I can leave peacefully, and she is coming with me, just a short ride. When I'm clear, I'll let her go. If I see anybody following me, I'll kill her, all eighteen years of her. You got that?"

"This is not you, Art. You can still survive this thing. You got out of Nam without a scratch...."

"and I'll get out of this, too. And if you want your deputy to go to work tomorrow, you tell him to come out from behind the house."

"Drop the shotgun, Billie, and come on out," I ordered. Billie threw the shotgun to the ground in front of him and walked out. Art fired one shot and dropped Billie. I reached for my weapon.

"Don't do it, Grant. I can best you with a pistol. Your deputy will live. He'll just have a sore knee for a while."

"Why did you shoot him, Art?"

"I didn't come back from Nam without a scratch, as you say I did, Grant. Some wounds don't need bandages, but they still leave nasty scars."

He took Elizabeth to the SHO and kept the .22 trained on me. I wasn't going to argue against his mastery with the pistol, but I couldn't let him take Elizabeth. Yet, I was helpless against his ability to handle that .22. Elizabeth looked down through me with eyes boring a hole in my heart. How was I going to get her out of this? I tried to assure her things would be all right. Norm said he would be here, but I saw no sign of State Troopers, a SWAT Team, or anything that would make me feel better.

Art backed the SHO down the driveway, headed for the road. As soon as he stopped to point the car in the direction he wanted to go, Elizabeth jumped out. She hit the ground hard and began to roll away from the car. Art fired one shot and caught her in the buttocks. Her escape forced Art to make the one mistake he should never have made, forgetting the essential rule of survival in Viet Nam; never hesitate. When he did, a volley of gunfire erupted. Like the scene from Bonnie and Clyde, when police fired on Clyde Barrow's car, putting 160 bullet holes in it from automatic weapons, a shotgun, and pistol fire. There was some irony in the killing of Art Williams. He, too, was driving a Ford at the time of the ambush.

I walked over to meet Norman and his troopers. "The man was either a fool or had a death wish. It didn't have to end this way." He looked at Elizabeth, asking,

"Are you alright little lady?"

"My butt is sore. I think he shot me. I feel something wet." Elizabeth ran her hand over her butt and brought back a red palm. She fainted in my arms, and I asked Norm to call for an ambulance. Billie was standing by the house with blood dripping down his pants leg.

"Does it hurt much, Billie?" I asked.

"Yeah, a little. I can't walk on it. And that was with a .22? I would hate to have anything bigger hit me."

"We'll get you and Elizabeth taken care of."

Norm told me a regular ambulance would take over an hour to reach us, so he called for a rescue chopper out of Sanford. It was there in ten minutes to take the two to Lakes Region General in Laconia. I told both of them I would see them tomorrow and told Elizabeth I would see her parents tonight and let them know where she was. Buster came with me to keep the kid's company as I talked to the parents. They were very understanding and appreciative that I made the trip over. I was back in Lakes Crossing before dark.

Norm left me a note saying he would send a deputy over to lend a hand while Billie was laid up.

He said he might find a secretary that would want a change of pace for a couple of weeks while Elizabeth was out. The bottom of the note read, "See you in the morning."

CHAPTER 35

Broken Glass

The cleaning person at the White House found broken glass on the floor in the hallway leading to the President's bedroom. He looked up and saw one window had been shot through and called security. They found three rounds of 7.62mm embedded in the opposite wall. The President was notified and called the Chief of Security to the Oval Office. James Oland knew what the call was about.

"Jimmy, come on in." The President is pacing, visibly shaken by the incident.

"I thought the windows in Residence were bulletproof. How could this have happened? Where could anyone be to make such a shot?"

"I'm sorry, Mr. President, but those windows weren't scheduled for replacement with bulletproof glass until tomorrow. I'll tell the crew on it today."

"Yes, please, but you must also find where the hell that shooter stood when he took the shot.

And then make arrangements to close off any other possible sites."

"Yes, Mr. President."

Comstock continued to pace the Oval Office. He is scared the next shot will be on him or his wife, like Snipes and his wife. Wondering where that next shot would come from, he cautiously goes to the windows and pulls the drapes closed, calling for VP Holloway to come to the office.

When the Vice President arrived, he found Comstock trying to move the Resolute desk away from the windows. Holloway called for assistance from anyone standing in the hallway. Secretary Cortez and Secretary White Feather walked by the Oval Office when asked to help the President move the desk. Watching the shameful spectacle, VP Holloway suggests to the President,

"Mr. President? Dan, why don't we sit down and discuss this before we accidentally destroy this handsome heirloom, this piece of our country's history."

Comstock stops pushing the desk; embarrassed, he looks at the three men, watching him.

"Oh, yes. I think you may be right. We should sit down and discuss this." The President moves to his chair and wipes his brow, perspiring.

"I know how this looks; the president has lost his mind. He's moving the furniture around in the Oval Office. Well, I'm not going crazy; I'm just concerned about that shooter, who is still out there. Do you know he shot through a window in my residence last night? My residence! Why he could have hit me!" Comstock yells.

Cortez and White Feather look at one another. They did not know the shooter was in Washington.

"Well, what have you two got to say about this? You stood before the whole of Congress, begging this crackpot assassin to stop the killing. Has he contacted you yet?"

"No, Mr. President, he hasn't," Cortez tells him.

"Well, then. Please take me to Camp David. He won't be able to get to me there, will he?"

"No, Mr. President, I think not," Holloway agrees.

Arrangements are made for President Comstock to arrive at Camp David the following afternoon. Secrecy is at its highest point, and the President is confident he will be safe there. Congress is told not to meet while the President is away. The President takes a window seat on the flight to Camp David. He orders the pilot of Marine 1 to climb a little higher, then turns to his secretary,

"They can't get me from here, can they?"

"I hope not, Mr. President, but I don't know how high an RPG will go," His secretary says in jest.

"That's not funny, Rebecca. Remember, if I go down, you go with me." He admonishes her.

"Yes, Mr. President," she apologizes. "It won't happen again."

"Yes, not if you want to keep your job," He adds.

A squad of Marines reports to the landing pad and informs the President the Camp has been swept and is safe. Comstock disembarks Marine 1. His nervousness causes him to scan the countryside on the ride in Cadillac 1.

"This thing is bulletproof. No one can get to me in here," he thinks.

Arriving at Camp David, Comstock's first stop is the bathroom. He closes the door and notices a sign tacked to the back of the door,

"Feeling Safe, Daniel?"

He feels faint and falls to the toilet seat, wetting his pants. He grabs the emergency cord calling for assistance. A male aide knocks on the door and asks,

"Are you alright, Mr. President? Do you need my help?"

"Yes," was all he could say. He pointed to his wet pants, then to the sign on the door. The aide calls Security and helps the President change from his wet clothes. Security goes on alert to investigate who tacked the sign on the bathroom door.

"I can't believe he got this close. He shot out my windows, and I thought that was close. Now, he's in my bathroom. What's next, the bedroom?" Comstock runs to his bedroom and draws back the sheets to find a note and a domino taped to the pillow. He begins screaming. The message on the pillow reads,

in worldwide, telling President Holloway they are eager to work with him. Domestically, House and Senate Chambers have indicated they are willing to sit down and renegotiate bills brought forth earlier and rejected by President Comstock. This is one for the books, Howard. Back to you in New York."

CHAPTER 36

The End And The Beginning

The front pages of every newspaper in the country and the world were filled with only two stories today. The most prominent story was,

**President Daniel Comstock Resigns, Article 25
Initiated, VP Holloway, Now President.**

The other big story and most probably more exciting was,

**Cabinet Assassin killed in Stand-off.
State Senator Implicated.**

My father had his fill of reading both stories and called me.
"Grant, you have to come down so we can celebrate."
"Celebrate what, dad?"
"Your birthday, son." he joked. "No! Come on, the capture and, fortunately, the elimination of the Cabinet assassin. It bothers me to think our own Senator Thomas Florin was involved. Wow!"

"I know, dad, but I'm not sure that calls for a celebration. I wouldn't mind meeting you at the Duck for a drink. Or better yet, dad. Why don't you come up here and see the beauty of my town, my new state? You would love it up here, and bring Veronica. I think she would genuinely enjoy New Hampshire. When can you come up?"

"I don't know, son. It's a long way.

"Dad. You can drive the Chrysler. It'll make it, and the folks up here would enjoy seeing a restored classic. There will be old cars from every generation lining both sides of Lakes Crossing this weekend, and a prize will be awarded for the oldest, the best restored, and the most accurately restored. Your Chrysler could take a prize home this weekend. Come on up and enjoy yourself. I've got room for you. You can stay in Buster's room."

"What? Stay in the dog's room?"

"I'm kidding, dad. I have an extra room you and Victoria will love. Stay the weekend and enjoy yourself."

Dad had a few days to make up his mind, close the firm, and pack for the weekend. He got the Chrysler ready for the two-hour trip and had Veronica get herself ready for a relaxing weekend. They arrived on Friday afternoon. Going out to meet them, I was stunned with gladness to see Rachel sitting in the back seat of that big convertible. All smiles from ear to ear; it was a Rachel I hadn't seen in a long time. She pulled off the silk scarf that kept her hair in order and let it fall to the ground, then greeted me with a kiss. I could see the glee of a little girl dancing in the rays of the summer sundown; her crystal blue marble eyes all lit up. It was the perfect ending, to a day that could have ended quite differently. The missing pieces of the life I left behind in the hustle and bustle of Rhode Island had come together in the quiet of nature and my New Hampshire home.

End

Thank You's

Dad…for giving me a deep sense of committment and a love and respect for the US Army, just as you maintained for the 30 years you served.

Mom…for showing what love is; the love you gave to us, your children, and dad.

Mimi…if God could have given me a better wife, he would have had to start all over again with a new Eve. All I have ia all you are. My Love forever.

My Children…surely a blessing to me from God. From you I learned patience and comedy. I'm not so sure we could share a serious moment. My love and dedication will go on till my clock runs out.

To the Men at Ruck-Up…I have never held such pride knowing you all have my '6 'covered.

To AJ…A Big Thank You. Amy was right sending me to you.

Let the Dominoes Fall is Bob's second book in three years. His first book, *Sittin' On A Headstone* is the story of a young man's growth into manhood, from simple beginnings in a small Rhode Island village to serving with the US Army through 18 months in the hell of Viet Nam as a helicopter doorgunner. The young man fights back from an horrendous wounding and deals with the not so subtle effects of PTSD. He survives the devastation of a divorce and the separation from his children, but makes it back to stable, happy life with another love.

Sittin' On a Headstone was a cathartic excersize in Bob's personal history. He was born in Pawtucket, R.I. on November 11, 1947, Veterans Day, joined the US Army at 18, learned to repair the Army's "Huey" helicopter and was wounded as a door gunner on June 5, 1968. He currently lives in the small town of Troy, NH, finding the peace to write and explore his imagination.